Francis Claudius Armstrong

The Naval Lieutenant

Vol. I

Francis Claudius Armstrong

The Naval Lieutenant
Vol. I

ISBN/EAN: 9783337020972

Printed in Europe, USA, Canada, Australia, Japan

Cover: Foto ©Andreas Hilbeck / pixelio.de

More available books at **www.hansebooks.com**

I.

In One Vol. Price 10s. 6d.

THE ADVENTURES OF A SERF WIFE

AMONG THE MINES OF SIBERIA.

II.

In Three Vols. Price 31s. 6d.

AN OLD MAN'S SECRET.

A Novel.

By FRANK TROLLOPE,

Author of " A Right-Minded Woman."

III.

In Three Vols. Price 31s. 6d.

IT MAY BE TRUE.

A Novel.

By MRS. WOOD.

IV.

In Three Vols. Price 31s. 6d.

TREASON AT HOME.

A Novel.

By MRS. GREENOUGH.

FAMILY MOURNING.

MESSRS. JAY

Would respectfully announce that great saving may be made by purchasing Mourning at their Establishment,

THEIR STOCK OF

FAMILY MOURNING

BEING

THE LARGEST IN EUROPE.

MOURNING COSTUME

OF EVERY DESCRIPTION

KEPT READY-MADE,

And can be forwarded to Town or Country at a moment's notice.

The most reasonable Prices are charged, and the wear of every Article Guaranteed.

THE LONDON

GENERAL MOURNING WAREHOUSE,

247 & 248, REGENT STREET,

(NEXT THE CIRCUS.)

JAY'S.

THE NAVAL LIEUTENANT.

A NAUTICAL ROMANCE.

IN THREE VOLUMES.

BY

F. C. ARMSTRONG,

Author of "The Two Midshipmen," "The Lily of Devon,"
"The Medora," "The Queen of the Seas," &c., &c.

VOL. I.

London:

T. CAUTLEY NEWBY, PUBLISHER,

30, WELBECK STREET, CAVENDISH SQUARE,

1865.

THE NAVAL LIEUTENANT.

CHAPTER I.

It was night, a dark and stormy night; the thunder of the cannon from the ramparts of Santa Cruz had ceased, not even the report of a musket broke upon the stillness; neither shouts of victory nor the cries of the wounded were to be heard; all was quiet, after several hours of a fierce and terrible cannonading.

The British fleet, under the command of a Trowbridge, and a Nelson, and other gallant officers, had stormed the almost impregnable fortress of Santa Cruz, and failed. The long line of mole, leading from the landing place to the great gate of the fortress, was literally strewed with English dead; there was not supposed to be one left alive of the heroic party that had attempted to storm the walls of the fortress.

When night closed the contest, the boats with the survivors of the attack returned to the fleet, and silence reigned in place of the terrible uproar that had filled the air during the period of conflict.

Amongst the heaps of dead covering the mole of Santa Cruz, wounded, but not very severely, lay the insensible body of a young officer of the Leander, fifty gun ship. Three times, after all his superior officers were slain, he had led his enraged and gallant followers to storm the gates; but showers of grape, and volleys of musketry, at pistol-shot distance, swept the mole incessantly—the iron shower mowing down his men; and when left almost alone, a musket shot in the shoulder and another striking him obliquely on the head, felled him insensible to the ground, and falling

near the edge of the mole, he rolled over,
pitching upon a heap of dead, thus escaping
a fall that otherwise might have perilled life
and limb.

Augustus Chamberlain, acting Lieutenant
of the Leander, the young officer who lay
stretched upon the dead, was at this period
scarcely more than nineteen, of a fine
athletic form, and more than prepossessing
features, remarkable for his gallantry, skill,
and knowledge of his profession; no wonder
that, with a generous and noble nature, he
became a favourite with his superior officers,
and the pet of the crews of the two ships in
which he had passed his six years of pro-
bation.

Having passed his examination, Captain
Thompson, of the Leander, an old friend of
his father's, who had died a post captain,
gave him the rank of Lieutenant, till his promotion could be confirmed by the Admiralty.

How long Augustus Chamberlain lay insensible he knew not, but it was dark when

he raised his head, which had been pillowed on the cold breast of a dead comrade. The night wind was sweeping over the blood-stained mole, and the wash of the sea,—breaking in a sullen murmur, as the tide rose close to the ill-fated dead,—roused him from his stupor, recollection gradually returned; and with a shudder, with difficulty he attained an upright posture. He felt dizzy and sick, as, wiping the blood from his face and eyes, he staggered on in the dark, till suddenly coming with considerable force against a black object, he fell over it and pitched into the bottom of a large boat, and, striking his head violently against an iron bolt, again relapsed into insensibility.

Rapidly the tide rose, and dashed against the sides of the boat, which soon floated, and the wild gusts of wind from the heights drove it from the beach ; once clear of the mole, it drifted rapidly out to sea, before a strong gale, and in a different direction from where the British ships lay at anchor.

When the young Lieutenant a second time recovered his senses, a summer night had passed away, and a dazzling sun threw its scorching rays over the white-topped seas; the clouds that had obscured the past night had vanished, and a clear, deep blue sky had succeeded.

It required but a moment, after conscious-ness returned, to satisfy our hero that he was once more on the element he loved; at first he imagined he had been rescued and carried on board his own ship, but a second glance around satisfied him that such was not the case. The open boat rolled and tossed, and plunged violently, as she at one time came broadside to the seas, or turned stern or stem to them, the spray flew over her, and Augustus Chamberlain was very soon con-vinced it would be necessary to get her be-fore the gale, or she would fill. So, rousing himself from his stupor, he raised himself, and, bending over the gunwale, bathed his head, wiped away the clotted blood from his eyes and face, and then took a survey of all around.

The boat had drifted about fifteen miles to sea during the hours of the night, but the lofty peak of Teneriffe still showed boldly an l grandly against the deep blue of the sky. Ship or boat he saw neither. The strong breeze curled the wave, and the dazzling sun sparkled on the crest. He looked anxiously over the boat, which he feared was a ship's long-boat. Neither mast nor sail could he see; but to his great joy there was one long oar jammed under the thwarts. In some measure regaining his strength, and always hopeful, he disengaged the oar, and perceiving some five or six yards of rope fastened to the ring in the bow of the boat, the remains of the painter, he cut it off, luckily having a knife in his pocket. His left arm was exceedingly sore, and almost useless, from the deep wound made by the musket ball, which, providentially had not lodged in the flesh. Nevertheless, he contrived to fasten the long oar to the stern of the boat, and, lashing it amidships, got the boat to steer dead before the breeze, and then baled the water out with a tin bread-case he found in the locker, with a jar of water, and a few soaked biscuits, which he placed out in the sun to dry, rejoicing that he had what would keep life in him, at all events for three or four days, and before that time expired he felt confident he should fall in with some ship.

As he sat gazing over the boundless sea stretched around, his thoughts reverted to the attack upon Santa Cruz, and, as he feared, the melancholy fate of his comrades. The second lieutenant who had the command of the storming party on the mole, he remembered, was killed in the very first discharge of grape-shot from the ramparts over the gate. The command then fell on himself; two brave young midshipmen, also, to his deep grief, met a gallant and early death. His party was then joined by the gallant Captain Bowen, of the Terpsichore, and his first lieutenant, both of whom perished together with all their men. From one of the officers our hero had heard that the Fox, cutter, with a crew of ninety-seven men, was sunk by the shot from the ramparts, and every soul on board had perished. It was with Captain Bowen's assistance that they were enabled to carry the mole head, which was defended by a thousand men, and six twenty-four pounders. Every possible disaster attended this most unfortunate expedition. It was here that Rear-Admiral Nelson lost his right arm.

All these matters floated through Augustus Chamberlain's brain as he sat buried in thought, gazing back in the direction of the bold peak of Teneriffe, till the shades of evening fell, and the short night threw a gloom over the still agitated deep. The island became lost to view. As our hero, tired and suffering much from his wounds, having ate a biscuit or two, and washed them down with a small quantity of water, threw himself on the stern sheets, and shortly, despite pain and distressing thoughts, fell into a troubled slumber.

A second day and second night passed, and only one vessel steering east met his gaze. Though he hoisted his coat on the oar, and held it aloft to attract attention, she stood away on her course, doubtless without perceiving him.

The last biscuit was consumed, and the last drop of water drank, and then our hero began to fear that he had a fearful fate before him. Help was, however, at hand, and with a heartfelt thanksgiving to Providence, he beheld a large bark steering direct for him, though he suspected he was not seen, in the dim light of a southern twilight, by those on board. In a few minutes it would be too dark to perceive him, though only twenty yards distant. But, providentially, the vessel was steering with all sail set direct for him. As soon as sufficiently near he hailed, shouting with all the strength he could muster; at the same time, seizing the oar, he

impelled the boat as much out of the direct
course of the ship as he could, for fear of
being run down. His hail was answered, and
the bark rounded to, almost rubbing the sides
of the boat, at the same time casting a rope
to him, which he caught and made fast to the
ring in the bows.

On being hauled alongside, he was questioned by one of the mates of the strange
ship, and, to his great joy, in his own language.
On stating that he was an English officer, he
was at once assisted on deck, and the boat,
which was a remarkably fine one, was also
hoisted on board. The captain came forward
and invited our hero to follow him into the
cabin, which he willingly did. The cabin of
the bark Sea Drift was large and comfortable. The vessel hailed from Liverpool, and
was bound to Bridgetown, Barbadoes.

Captain Henderson was extremely kind and
attentive to the young officer, had his wounds
well washed and dressed by one of his passengers, a young surgeon, going out to Barba-

does to better his fortunes. As soon as this was done, and he had partaken of some refreshment, our hero retired to rest, completely worn out, after five days of great privation and no little suffering.

There were six or eight passengers on board the Sea Drift, residents on the island, and all planters. Augustus Chamberlain's fine person and handsome features greatly interested them, and all were anxious to know how he came to be adrift in an open boat, on the wide ocean, without provisions or water, and no other help than an oar to guide or manage his craft. Captain Henderson would not allow his guest to be questioned the previous night, for he perceived that he was greatly exhausted, and suffering from two severe wounds. However, the next day, after a hearty breakfast, he satisfied the curiosity of the party assembled at the breakfast-table.

Two of the planters, wealthy slave-owners on the island, requested our hero to make their residences his home whilst he remained

in Barbadoes, and offered him any assistance
in money or anything else he might require.
All were extremely sorry to hear of the
failure of the attack on Teneriffe, and grieved
to think that such men as Nelson and Trowbridge should have suffered so severe a defeat.

After a pleasant voyage, the Sea Drift ran
into Bridgetown harbour, and Mr. Joyce, a
bachelor, and a most hospitable man, insisted on our hero's taking up his residence
with him— having a large mansion in the
town.

After thanking Captain Henderson, and
distributing amongst the crew all the cash he
had in his pocket, he went ashore and took
up his abode with Mr. Joyce, intending to
take his departure in the first ship-of-war
bound for great Britain, that should touch at
the island.

Our hero found no difficulty in getting a
supply of cash, through the introduction and
kindness of Mr. Joyce, and having a change
of dress made, and his wounds getting per-

fectly cured, he determined to see as much
of the island as he could ere leaving.

One day, rambling along the sea shore,
some few miles from the town, he came to an
abrupt point, barring all further progress.
He looked up at the cliff above him, rising
to eighty or ninety feet, rather precipitous,
but still possible of ascent. Rather than
turn back, he commenced climbing the height,
and after a sharp struggle, gained the summit.
He then perceived, on looking around, that
he had trespassed into a fine plantation, and
before him was a very handsome mansion,
with its lawn in front, and a broad, well-rolled
avenue leading from the house door in a
serpentine form to where he stood, and turning off, continued to a lodge gate, some two
hundred feet further down the walk. Whilst
he stood admiring the place, and the beauty
of the various plants and shrubs bordering
the avenue, he perceived a young lady
mounted on a seemingly high-spirited jennet,
which she was restraining as if waiting for a

gentleman who stood conversing with a lady on the doorsteps, whilst two negroes were holding a couple of saddle horses. Seeing that he was intruding on private property, our hero was about to return the way he came, but just then the young girl, tired of curbing her spirited steed, waved her hand to the gentleman, let her impatient animal have the reins, and away down the avenue he galloped at a quick pace.

Augustus Chamberlain was particularly struck with the grace and elegance with which the girl managed her steed, and waited a moment longer. Just then the animal trod upon a sharp stone, and stumbled. The sudden jerk, and the rider looking round at the moment, nearly unhorsed her, causing her to lose her hold of the reins. Perhaps the animal was frightened, or wild at feeling himself free, for he at once tossed his head, neighed fiercely, and plunging into a mad gallop, cleared the ornamental fence between the avenue and the precipice, and the next moment, with his fair burden, would have plunged over the cliff, had not the strong hand of our hero seized the bridle, and, by a powerful jerk, forced the animal back on its haunches, on the very edge of the precipice. Catching the falling girl in his arms, but staggering with the impetus and the great exertion he had used, he lost his balance, and over the precipice he went, just having time and strength to push the girl back before he fell. Over our hero went, bringing a considerable amount of earth and stones with him, whilst the girl, her hat knocked off, her hair streaming wildly in the sea breeze, uttered a wild, piercing cry, changing to a shriek. She gazed over the edge, expecting to see her preserver dashed to the bottom and killed. But Augustus, accustomed to accidents of all sorts, had been alive to the fate that awaited him, could he not by some means break his fall ; he first grasped a goodly-sized shrub growing out of a fissure of the rock. This, though

it gave way, checked his rapid descent, but he
came with great violence against a projecting
mass of rock.   He was much bruised, and his
left arm benumbed by the shock, but he nevertheless took a steady grip of the projecting
rock, and finally arrested his progress down-
wards, and then lay quite helpless on a small
projecting ledge, thirty feet from the summit.
His first thought was to look up, and his eyes
rested upon the pale, anxious face of the girl,
gazing down at him.

"God be praised," she uttered aloud, "he
is not killed! he is looking up at me!" and
she waved her hand, crying out, "hold fast;
help is coming."

"Do not be alarmed," he returned.   "I'm
all right, only I cannot get up again without
assistance."

"Ah!   Thank God! here is papa, and
help," and the next moment he beheld a
gentleman anxiously gazing down at him, and
also the faces of half a dozen negroes, uttering
all manner of strange gibberings.

"Do not move," shouted the gentleman, "you are on a very slight and narrow ledge; there are ropes coming; any bones broken?"

"No, I fancy not," replied our hero, "but I cannot very well use either my right leg or my left arm."

"Ah!" exclaimed the girl, clasping her hands. "He is greatly hurt; oh! papa, but for him, I should have been dashed to pieces, what could have made Rollo do so wicked a thing—"

"How grateful ought we to be to Providence," said the gentleman, turning to a lady who just then arrived, and, clasping her daughter in her arms, burst into a flood of tears.

In the meantime four Negroes returned with ropes and a large easy chair.

"Can you fasten the rope round your waist," asked the stranger from above, "or shall the chair be lowered?"

"No occasion for anything but a rope, I'm a sailor, and well know how to use it."

"Good Heaven," returned the Englishman, "half my wealth would not pay for the service you have rendered us."

A stout coil of rope was lowered, but not one of the chattering negroes would attempt the descent even with assistance of the rope—

"Well," thought our Hero, "here's a nice mess I am in—shall not be able to use my leg for a month—and am not certain that my thigh is not broken; but I would run the same risk again for that sweet little face."

Having fastened the rope round his waist, and steadied himself with a grasp of his right hand, he called out to those above to haul up gently, helping himself as well as he could, and fending off the rocks with his left leg when he swung against a projecting one. He at length reached the top, and four stout negroes caught him in their arms, and placed him at once in the easy chair, giving him a considerable amount of pain, in doing so. The girl, who was not more than fifteen, at once caught his hand in hers, and, with the tears streaming down her pale but exquisitely lovely face, said,

"Oh, Sir, you have saved my life, and nearly killed yourself."

"No, my dear young lady," replied our hero. " I have a great deal of life in me yet, and would risk a dozen lives to save so sweet a face from harm," and kissing the small fair hand that held his so tightly, he looked up into the gentleman's handsome features who was gazing at him most earnestly.

" I really, sir—and the brow too—pardon me for thinking at such a moment, but your extraordinary resemblance to a dear old friend amazes me ; but now let us to the house, a surgeon will be here directly," and the negroes at once lifting the chair, and followed by the gentleman and his wife and daughter, proceeded to the house.

CHAPTER II.

BEFORE the arrival of the doctor, Augustus Chamberlain had been undressed and placed in bed in one of the most comfortable chambers of Mr. Mortimer's house, and a messenger had also been sent to inform his kind host, Mr. Joyce, of the accident, as he would be alarmed.

It chanced that very day that a man-of-war brig, the Dasher, had put into Port Royal on her way to England, and would sail again in a day or two. Our hero, was, however, much more seriously hurt than he was aware of, and after a critical examination by the doctor, the latter said that "Owing to his robust and strong frame, and great exertion in saving himself, he had escaped breaking any bones, but he was much bruised, and his right leg and thigh so severely wounded that a month or two must elapse before he could expect to walk well, or be able to exert himself."

The invalid was annoyed.

" You do not know my constitution, Mr. Belmont," he said ; " besides, we sailors are so accustomed to be knocked about, and take so little pains to cure ourselves, that I feel sure I shall be able to move about in a week."

" My dear young gentleman," answered Mr. Belmont, with a smile, " if you attempt any such thing you will walk lame for the rest of your life."

Mr. Mortimer, a keen reader of the human countenance, saw what was passing in the young lieutenant's mind.

Pressing his hand, he said, with much emotion—

" You are thinking, my dear sir, that you are troublesome to us. You, who have saved the treasure of our lives. Let this house be your home, and every soul in it will testify by attention and kindness the deep gratitude that we owe you. You have escaped a frightful death, even if you had not saved our child. What we do for you is a very poor return for the services rendered us seventeen years ago by your father, Captain John Chamberlain, of the Racehorse, whose son I am sure you are."

Our hero looked amazed; but the doctor recommending quiet for a few days, at least, Mr. Mortimer acquiesced, and promised very soon to make him fully acquainted with his early friendship with his father.

Our hero, though he chafed at confinement, and bitterly lamented not being able to sail in the man-of-war brig for England, could not but be sensible of the extraordinary kindness lavished on him, not only by the attendants, but by Mr. and Mrs. Mortimer. The young girl, whose lovely features haunted his memory, was for a few days confined to her room, having slightly sprained her ankle, but she sent her love to him every day, and all the books she could think of for him to read, promising, the moment she was able, to come and see him.

"She is only a child," said our hero to himself, musing, "her father is almost a millionaire. In a year or two Annie Mortimer will be a dangerous companion for a poor lieutenant. By Jove, I do not consider I have a right now, as far as my feelings are concerned, but they do say that midshipmen are always in love, and I can scarcely call myself a lieutenant yet; and, faith, a lieutenant is quite as susceptible as a midshipman. It's only when you get to be post-captain that you can consider yourself safe, and, by Jove, one rarely gets that rank till the heart grows cold."

Our impatient hero left his bed before the week expired, sitting in an easy chair by the window, his leg propped up on cushions, and a table loaded with books and delicacies of all kinds beside him. As he gazed out on the lovely view before him, Mrs. Mortimer and her daughter entered the room. Augustus made a movement as if inclined to rise; but Annie Mortimer, with anxiety vividly expressed in her youthful features, ran to his side, and, with all the freedom of extreme youth, pressed her hand upon his arm, to keep him quiet, saying, whilst her eyes sparkled with delight,

" Oh, I am so glad, so very glad, to see you up; it gives me such pleasure, you cannot think. I have been fretting about you ever since my naughty Rollo behaved so badly. I have scolded her well for her wickedness."

Our hero took the little white hand in his, and, for his life, he could not help kissing it, though he blushed as he did so, and his eyes rested on Mrs. Mortimer's countenance; but there he saw naught but a pleased and happy smile, as she came and sat down on the sofa beside him, saying,

" Annie has been longing to come and see you ; and indeed it rejoices us all to have you up, and I trust before a fortnight expires you will be able to walk."

"Oh, dear madam, with such care as I have had long before that I hope. I am sure I can never be sufficiently grateful for all the kindness I have experienced here."

"It would have been a desolate home, but for your courage," said Mrs. Mortimer, earnestly. "Mr. Mortimer is anxious to have a long chat with you. He has been, and is still, so very busy preparing everything for our return immediately to England, that he is seldom at home during the day. I expect in a month we shall be able to sail for Great Britain."

"Ah! not for a month," said Annie Mortimer, eagerly. "Well, Mr. Chamberlain," she continued, looking our hero earnestly in the face, "You must get well soon. I so much want to show you all the beautiful rides and walks about this place; you cannot think how lovely they are. You were never here before, I believe?"

" No, never, Miss Mortimer," returned the invalid, " and a wonderful chance brought me here now."

" Ah!" said Annie, seriously, " it was not chance, but Providence; was it not, mamma?"

" Yes, my love, most providential. Ah, there is little Henry calling out lustily; I must bid you good bye for awhile."

" Do bring him here, Mrs. Mortimer, I do so love children."

Little Henry was brought in by the nurse, and a fine little fellow he was, with his curly brown hair and blue eyes. He was about eleven months old.

How strange, but how true it is, that infants and children take wonderful likings and dislikings, even at first sight. Our hero was sincere in saying he wished the child to be brought in; he was fond of children, and had such winning ways that 'the smallest child would at once smile, and hold out its little hands to be taken, and so it was with little Harry. He at once became delighted, and laughed and crowed in boisterous glee, when played with and caressed by our hero. In fact, all became so intimate and pleasant together that a couple of hours passed away without being heeded, so that, when parting, Annie said, with all the artlessness of fifteen, as she placed her fair little hand in our hero's, to bid him good bye, " I will tell you what you must do, you must call me Annie, and I will call you Augustus. We shall be like brother and sister, shall we not, mamma. Do you agree to that?"

" Most assuredly I do," said our hero, with some emotion, as he looked into the young girl's lovely blue eyes.

This contract was carried out on one side, strictly ; but we fear before the month was out, the lieutenant was fast sinking the brother into the lover, notwithstanding the extreme youth of Annie Mortimer.

A day or two after this, Mr. Mortimer came in the evening to sit for a couple of hours with his young guest.

After some preliminary conversation on un-important subjects, Mr. Mortimer said, " I have been so very busy, my dear young friend, with winding up my affairs, and finally dis-posing of my property in this island, that I have had no time to enter into any lengthened conversation with you ; you are now so very much better, that I can talk without disturb-ing you.

" In the first place, let me hear how you came to be placed in the situation you are, alone on this Island; for I very imperfectly heard Mr. Joyce's account; and, after the im-mense service you have rendered me, I wish, not only from that circumstance, but from others which I will by-and-bye state, to be a true and lasting friend to you, in fact a second father, for you have deeply interested me."

" My dear Mr. Mortimer," said our hero, much moved by his host's impressive manner and words. " You overrate the service I chanced to perform—a service any man would have done, had be been where I was at the time."

" Let that be," interrupted Mr. Mortimer, allowing his hand to rest in our hero's, and pressing it. " Now give me a little history of yourself, and then perhaps I may tell you something you do not know of your parents."

The young man said, with a smile, " My life, my dear sir, has been one of little consequence as yet, and my adventures of no great moment."

Our hero then related all he knew about himself and family, and of his short career in the navy, up to the landing at Santa Cruz, and arrival in Barbadoes.

" Well, my young friend," said Mr. Mortimer, " though you have kept your own exploits pretty well in the back ground, still, for a youth of nineteen or twenty, I think you have had your share of perils by sea and perils by land. It seems you have not heard who your mother was, and though I knew a great deal about your good father, once my

most esteemed friend, I can only tell you of
your mother, that she was a lady of rank, and
although your father was of as good a family
as any in Suffolk, yet so vindictively was he
treated by your mother's high-born relations,
that he never, after six months of his marriage, mentioned their names. They even tried
to draw him from his profession, but there
they failed ; he f ll upon the deck of his own
ship, in the moment of a glorious victory, and
left an untarnished name to posterity, a
name and fame his only son may be proud
o .

"I will now state how my intimacy with
your father commenced; first of all, we formed
a friendship at school; oftentimes those boyish
friendships last as long as life.   Such was the
case with your father and myself.

" Your father was placed on board a man-of-
war at the age of fourteen. We parted vowing
a firm friendship.   Shortly after, I sailed for
this island, in which my father owned extensive plantations, as well as property, in

Jamaica. I lost my mother when very young, and was but three and twenty when I succeeded my father in his large property in this island, and elsewhere. After a year or so I visited England, married the daughter of a worthy clergyman in Kent, and two years after sailed with my wife and Annie, a baby of fourteen months old, for Barbadoes. Two other children were born to us, but neither survived beyond a year or so; years passed away, and Annie became the idol of our hearts, for we thought we should have no more children.

"I had often heard of your father and his gallant actions, and his promotion to be captain of a frigate. In the year 1780, this island was visited by the most awful hurricane on record. Above four thousand persons perished in this awful visitation. Some few weeks before this terrible calamity your father's ship, the Racehorse, entered the port. You may imagine how rejoiced we were to meet again; he became our cherished guest,

for at school he had twice saved my life. He
told me he had been married, and was then a
widower, and that he had left his only child,
about four or five years older than our Annie,
under the charge of a most excellent, kind-
hearted woman, the widow of a master's
mate.

"The night of that awful hurricane, Captain
Chamberlain, with a number of his sailors,
were on shore; fortunately, the Racehorse
frigate had put to sea for a short cruise the
day before. I shall not attempt to describe
to you the horrors that followed; suffice to say
that our roof was blown into the sea,
all our out-offices destroyed, our plantations
torn up; and, finally, a fearful fire raged in
our dwelling-house. We should all have
perished but for the arrival of Captain
Chamberlain and his brave men. He himself
carried my wife out of the burning house,
previous to which I had been knocked sense-
less by the falling of a beam. Two of his
men, after a terrible struggle, saved me,

together with my darling child. Thus we all owed our lives to your gallant father, who, with several of his brave sailors, was severely burnt. The house we are now in was built on the ruins of our old dwelling.

"This is not all we owed to your noble father, who was nearly three years on this station. A ship of mine, with a cargo worth one hundred and fifty thousand pounds, was captured by the French frigate, the Furieux. The Racehorse gave chase to her, and after a desperate engagement with her and a French gun-brig, recaptured my ship, and brought her and the French gun-brig into harbour. In this action he was so severely injured that he was brought ashore, and, of course, to our dwelling. He was nearly two months recovering.

"I tell you this, my dear young friend, briefly and simply, to bring you as quickly as possible to the chief object of this conversation. One evening before your father's final departure from Barbadoes I said to him,

' John, I have one thing deeply at heart, and on you depends the realising of this wish.'

" ' Well, Henry,' he answered, ' if it depends on me, your object may be said to be accomplished. Now what is it ?'

" I replied, ' you have a son some four years older than my daughter.' (Our hero felt his cheek blush, and perhaps his pulse beat faster; but Mr. Mortimer continued). ' I wish, if God spares us all, the bonds of friendship, strong as they are, should be doubly strengthened by the union of our two dear children.'

" ' What!' " exclaimed Captain Chamberlain, with much emotion; ' you, a millionaire, give your only child to the almost penniless son of a poor sailor ! '

" I took his hand. ' John,' said I, ' you agreed to grant my wish; therefore, I consider that settled. So don't talk to me of millionaires and poor sailors.'

" It will be sufficient to tell you, my dear young friend," continued Mr. Mortimer,

" that, before Captain Chamberlain sailed, we settled everything to our mutual satisfaction. Alas! he never reached his native land. He died in battle, just as the flag of a gallant enemy was hauled down, as a token of surrender, after a furious contest of seven hours. This I did not know for eighteen months. I was even then preparing for my return to England, but so extensive were my mercantile connections and affairs, that time was required to wind up my accounts and dispose of my property in the two islands.

" When I heard of your dear father's death, I immediately wrote to my solicitor in London, a gentleman in whom I have unbounded confidence, requesting him to at once find you out, and to spare no expense in perfecting your education, and on no account to let you be placed in the navy.

" For more than a year I did not learn that the packet carrying the mails was captured by one of the enemy's ships, and heard from another source that you were a midshipman.

"So you may imagine my surprise and joy when I discovered, in the person of my child's deliverer, the very person I was so anxiously inquiring about.

"Some eleven months ago my beloved wife presented me with a son and heir, several years having intervened between his and my daughter's birth. This again delayed our departure; but we are now in a fair way of being ready to embark for England in six or eight weeks. By that time the Cumberland Packet will take us all to England, and during those six weeks I trust you will see enough of my dear little girl to make you contented in complying with your dear father's wish and mine."

"Oh! Mr. Mortimer, you overpower me," said our hero, enthusiastically, "with such princely generosity. For me to aspire to the hand of your daughter appears—"

"Nay, not one word about that," interrupted Mr. Mortimer. "You are both extremely young, and I feel convinced that the

more you know, the more you will learn to es-
teem and love each other.

"I have kept you conversing long enough
and will leave you to think over all I have
said, so that when next we resume the subject
you will have made up your mind to become
my son-in-law in a couple of years," and he
affectionately pressed our hero's hand.

The young lieutenant returned the pressure,
overwhelmed with astonishment at this most
unexpected and unexampled good fortune thus
pressed upon him.

A fortnight passed ere our hero was enabled
to walk about the plantation, his companion
generally Annie Mortimer, as attentive to him
as the fondest sister could be. Little Henry
took a wonderful fancy to him, and he gam-
bolled on the grass with the child, played
with him, and carried him about for two
hours. When quite recovered, the young
lieutenant rode out with mother and daughter,
rambled over the romantic scenery that sur-
rounded the mansion, made great friends of

the simple-minded, affectionate negroes, who all loved their kindmaster, and shed tears at being restored to liberty; for not one of his many slaves would Mr. Mortimer sell.

CHAPTER III.

On the tenth December, the Cumberland packet, armed, having a letter of marque, commanded by Captain Peter Inglis, sailed from Barbadoes for Liverpool with a valuable cargo and several chief cabin and some steerage passengers. Amongst the chief cabin passengers were Mr. and Mrs. Mortimer and family and servants—they occupied the two state rooms. Our hero and four gentlemen occupied the rest of the sleeping accommodation.

A most devoted love for her affianced husband had crept into Annie Mortimer's young and guileless heart. Young as she was, with all her childish manner and simplicity,

this new feeling absorbed all others. The
young sailor, too, became passionately attached
to his lovely companion, and Mr. and Mrs.
Mortimer beheld this love springing into being
in their young hearts, with a feeling of intense
satisfaction. Thus, with joyful anticipation
of a prosperous voyage, and of a happy, tranquil home when settled in their native land,
they embarked for England.

Alas! we may hope, we may anticipate, and
build fabrics of happiness, and paint pictures
of joyful homes, and dream of undisturbed
felicity; all to be dissipated and destroyed by
circumstances never contemplated.

The weather at starting was fine, and the
sea smooth and tranquil.

Captain Inglis, a skilful seaman, kind and
courteous to his passengers, introduced them
all to each other as they sat down to the
dinner table the first day after leaving port.
There is only one of the passengers we need
particularly describe, for he has much to do
with the personages of our story hereafter.

This person stated, on taking his passage, that he was a French nobleman, obliged to quit his country in order to save his head. In consequence of his devotion to the Royal family, he had become a marked man, and after incredible dangers had escaped from France in a vessel bound to Cuba, from Cuba he got to Barbadoes, and was now on his voyage to England, there to watch the progress of affairs in France. He possessed, he said, abundant funds, supplied to him by certain parties, who had contrived to obtain possession of his estates, in trust for him till better times. He called himself the Count de Maule; he was a tall, and rather well-looking man of about thirty-three years of age, spoke very little English, but made great efforts to render himself agreeable to the ladies, by performing all those small attentions at which Frenchmen are so *au fait.*

To Miss Mortimer he would, had it been possible, have been most attentive, but she evidently disliked even speaking to him; and our hero, before six days had expired, most cordially disliked, and moreover had a very despicable opinion of, the Frenchman, the reason for which will be explained hereafter.

After a very tolerable but tedious passage, The Cumberland, by no means a fast sailer, arrived within sight of the Spanish coast. Captain Inglis had endeavoured to get as near as possible to the coast of Ireland, in order to avoid French cruisers and French privateers, but baffling and contrary winds had kept him more to the southward than he liked but a shift of wind enabled him at length to steer for the coast of Ireland.

On the first of January, the weather thick and blowing stiffly, Captain Inglis considered he was then about ten leagues from the mouth of the Shannon, when the fog lifting, shewed him a large schooner lying to about four miles to the westward of him.

Our hero was walking the deck, with Annie Mortimer, carefully muffled for the breeze was cold. When the vessel was first

observed, Captain Inglis's glass was on her
in a moment, and then, handing the glass to
our hero, he said,

"I don't like the look of that schooner,
what do you think of her?"

Our hero took the glass, and after a steady
look, said calmly,

"She is letting draw her fore sheet, she's
a privateer."

"A Privateer!" exclaimed Annie, with a
start, "you do not mean that she is a French
privateer!"

"Do not be alarmed, dearest," he whispered,
"we are quite able to take care of ourselves
if she be; you had better go down below, we
are going to tack, and the breeze is freshening."

"Good gracious," she continued, turning
a little pale, "you surely will not have to
fight."

Augustus reassured his companion, and led
her below; then all the male passengers came
upon deck.

Captain Inglis, his mate, our hero, with another English officer, a passenger, a Lieut. Gorlius, were standing together, watching the stranger vessel, which suddenly altered her course, and stood direct for the Cumberland.

"Faith, there's nothing like being prepared," said Captain Inglis, " she is a splendid schooner, above two hundred tons, but whether English or French, I cannot say."

"She is French built at all events," interposed our hero, " she may be a prize taken by some of the cruisers, but as we have shewn our bunting, it's rather strange she shews none; but she sails marvellously fast. I do not see above half a dozen hands upon her deck."

" Depend upon it, Augustus," remarked Mr. Mortimer, anxiously, " she's a French privateer."

" Well, if so, my dear sir," replied Captain Inglis, speaking cheerfully, and rubbing his hands, " we can, I am happy to say, give him a warm reception, if he is inclined to try our metal."

The Cumberland had a crew of men and boys, thirty-five in all, four 12-pounders and two swivels, mounted on each quarter. The guns had all been shotted the previous day, and the men now turned up armed with cutlass and pistol. Our hero, Lieut. Gorlins, and Mr. Mortimer, and three steerage passengers all eagerly offered their assistance, and received arms, in case of need.

The wind was blowing fresh; and to windward there seemed a thick bank of fog, coming directly down upon them. Augustus Chamberlain suddenly seized Captain Inglis's arm, and exclaimed.—" She is French and full of men; there's no time to lose; she sees this fog coming, and will run us on board without firing a shot; let us be prepared."

Captain Inglis started, but at once requested our hero to select the best and youngest men to repel the attempt to board. The next instant the schooner ran up her flag, and fired a shotted gun, which knocked a whole shower of splinters out of the bowsprit, cutting away the stay, and letting the gib fly loose. Bang went the two twelve pounders of the Cumberland, and the next instant the privateer, with her decks crowded, ran her on board, pitching grapnels into her rigging.

The Cumberland was a high ship, and the schooner, though a longer vessel, was very low, so that the men in the latter had to scramble over the bulwarks to get to the deck of the former.

Whilst several of the Cumberland's men hurried to cut away the grapnels, our hero, with his twenty stout, active, and picked crew, gave the enemy so severe a lesson with cutlass and pistol that the first boarders were hurled back upon the deck of the schooner; many wounded, and three killed. Exasperated at this repulse, the captain, a short, but very powerful man, shouted to his men, and cheered them to a second attack. There were more than sixty men in the privateer. She had eight large guns, and a swivel amidships. By this time the dense fog came sweeping over the agitated sea, bringing a strong wind with it.

The captain of the privateer had gained the deck, when Augustus Chamberlain faced him, cutlass in hand. Whilst Captain Inglis. Lieutenant Gorlins, and Mr. Mortimer were driving the boarding party over the bows, and casting off the grapnels, a fierce fight took place between our hero and the privateer captain.

It was at that moment that Annie Mortimer, fearfully excited, and trembling for her father's and her lover's life, contrived to gain the cabin stairs, and gaze out over the blood-stained deck of the Cumberland.

With a look of intense anxiety she beheld her lover cast the man he was fighting with against the bulwark, whilst the mate of the privateer, rushing up, fired his pistol at the young lieutenant's head. Uttering a cry of horror Annie, involuntarily sprang on deck, but her lover remained unhurt, and the next instant he hurled the privateer captain over the side ; as he did so, a violent squall struck the two vessels, and a dense fog enveloped both, whilst the wind and the breaking of the grapnels and chains forced the two vessels asunder, and so dense was the fog that in less than five minutes they were invisible to each other, though the enraged privateers fired several guns in the direction they supposed the Cumberland to be. But Captain Inglis had at once braced round the yards, and stood away for the Irish coast.

Augustus Chamberlain, with one or two sharp cutlass wounds, had rushed to the side of Annie, and at once hurrying her, half fainting below, gave her to the care of her terrified mother. Having pacified the females by stating that there was no further danger, the privateer having been beaten off, he returned upon deck. Captain Inglis shook him heartily by the hand, saying " Your spirited conduct and desperate attacks upon the boarders and the hurling the privateer skipper over the side has saved the ship. I regret to say we have two men killed, and seven injured, Lieut. Gorlins slightly wounded from a pistol shot, and Mr. Mortimer with a flesh wound."

Three of the privateer's men remained prisoners on board the Cumberland. One was the second mate of the schooner. The prisoners were in a high state of excitement, swearing that the crew of the Cumberland should pay dearly for their temporary success, which they declared they owed entirely to the coming on of the fog. They, however, grew calmer after some hours' confinement, and then they stated that the schooner was the much feared and celebrated privateer Belle Poule, which hailed from Brest.

This privateer had done immense mischief to English merchant vessels, and had hitherto baffled the fastest British cruisers. Her captain, Jacques Belot Brossac, was notorious for his savage cruelty and desperate courage.

Captain Inglis hoped to get close in with the Irish coast the following day, and thus avoid any more French cruisers or privateers. But, unfortunately, none on board the Cumberland were aware that they were running into the lion's mouth; for at this period a French fleet was attempting the invasion of Ireland. This expedition, however, met with a most disastrous fate.

During the short contest with the privateer, the female passengers had remained in the cabin in a state of intense agitation. Mrs. Mortimer, trembling for the safety of her husband, and clasping her darling boy to her bosom; whilst all feared captivity. Amongst the group, however, was the French emigrant the Count de Maule. He looked exceedingly pale and excited; still he made several efforts to be attentive to Mrs. and Miss Mortimer, lamenting his hard fate that he could not fight against his countrymen, and saying it was trying to his feelings to see other men gallantly defending their ship, whilst he was forced to remain inactive.

From the very commencement of the voyage, Annie Mortimer had taken a most peculiar dislike to this man. Constantly, when he had an opportunity, he addressed her, and he was continually keeping his eyes fixed upon her, with a strange expression, extremely disagreeable to her. She would have noticed this to her mother and to our hero; but, young as she was, she had become aware how naturally fiery the temper of her betrothed was, and how enraged he would be, if he only knew the Frenchman annoyed her. She kept her thoughts, therefore, to herself concerning the Count de Maule, knowing how short a time she would be subject to his disagreeable manner.

Mrs. Mortimer, too, had very little belief in the Count's pretensions to being one of the French noblesse; she strongly suspected he was playing a part; when, therefore, he began lamenting his fate, and not being able to assist the gallant defenders of the ship in driving away the privateer, she said, quietly—

"Surely, Monsieur, as a loyal subject of the Bourbons, you ought to feel as great a desire to haul down the tri-colour as anyone on board this ship."

The Count looked disconcerted, and was stammering out some sort of apology, when a loud and triumphant cheer from the crew of the Cumberland, was so significant of victory, that the ladies felt ready to join in it, whilst the Count started up and rushed upon deck.

Whilst every attention was being paid to the wounded, the ladies humanely offering their services, Capt. Inglis and his crew were busy repairing damages, splicing rigging, and replacing the running rigging, and getting the ship ready to face a gale, which was evidently coming on. There was no fear of the privateer, for the fog was so dense that, standing by the helm, the bowsprit of the ship was invisible.

Augustus Chamberlain made very light indeed of the two or three cutlass wounds he had received; having washed and bandaged the worst, he gave all his attention and care to his beautiful betrothed, whilst nursing the little boy, who doted on him, and would scarcely quit his arms to go to his nurse.

Mr. Mortimer sat by his beloved partner's side, recounting to her the particulars of the fight, and enthusiastically declaring they owed their safety to our hero, for had not the privateer's skipper been checked in his attempt to board, the swarm of men that were following him would have swept the deck of the Cumberland. Alas! in the joy of their hearts at escaping from perhaps a long captivity, they never calculated or thought of what the morrow might bring. During the night it blew very hard, almost a gale, and the fog continued, the packet standing in for the Irish coast under treble-reefed topsails. Before morning, it began to rain heavily, and just as the dawn made, Capt. Inglis and our hero went on deck. There was a very rough sea, and the Cumberland, having a heavy cargo, laboured considerably, but being a strongly built ship, she stood the shocks of the head seas bravely.

"It blew hard during the night, Captain," said our hero to the skipper, "there is more sea up now than this breeze warrants."

"I expect we had only the tail end of the gale," returned Capt. Inglis, "and I think before long we shall have the wind into the north-west. The fog, I fancy, is lifting."

"This heavy rain," said the young lieutenant, will cause a change. I wonder where La Belle Poule is. I should like to take that privateer; I heard of several of her exploits just before we left England in the——"

"Do you see how it is clearing towards the nor'west?" remarked the skipper.

In less than twenty minutes the fog began to change its direction, the clouds to break, and the easterly wind to lull. Ten minutes more, and the sky opened clearly to the north, the breeze

suddenly, in a strong blast, threw the topsails against the mast, the rain ceased, and a
strong squally nor'wester scattered the white
tops of the seas over the agitated waters.

" A sail, ho !" shouted the man on the look-
out,

" Where away ?" asked the skipper.

All hands looked anxiously in the nor'west
quarter, where the sail was indicated by the
look out. All thought of La Belle Poule, but
one look through the glass, and the skipper,
handing it to our hero, said, " It's a very large
ship, probably one of our two deckers. See,
the land is distinctly visible, and no French
vessel of that size would hug the Irish
coast."

Our hero, who was by no means satisfied
that the skipper's assertion was correct,
ascended to the main-top, and then bent
the glass upon the strange ship which was
rapidly approaching them. Very few minutes'
observation satisfied him that the stranger
was a gun ship running out from the Irish

coast, and no doubt steering direct towards them, but whether English or French he could not say. If French, their fate was decided. Feeling deeply anxious, he descended to the deck.

" Well, my dear sir, what do you think of her? She comes rapidly up with us."

" She's a seventy-four, Captain, and I fear French."

" Good heaven! then our capture is certain," said the skipper despondingly, " there is not another craft in sight. It is not usual for a seventy-four of the enemy to be cruising so close in with the Irish coast. I will alter our course, however, and see if she will notice us."

With the British ensign flying at her peak, the Cumberland altered her course, tacking in for Three Castle Head, which could now be distinctly seen with the glass. Almost immediately the seventy-four hauled to the wind, and stood right across the course of the packet; at the same time the tri-colour flew out from her mizen peak, and a wreath of smoke curled out from her starboard bow, whilst the boom of a heavy gun, shotted, pealed over the deep, sending dismay into many a heart on board the Cumberland.

The captain turned with a deeply chagrined countenance, and said to our hero, who was looking very serious.

" It's all up with us; flight is useless."

"Perfectly so," returned Augustus Chamberlain. " Still hope is not lost, we may expect to fall in with an English ship of war before yonder ship can carry us into port. I will go below and break this sad news to our passengers."

Mrs. Mortimer and Annie were overwhelmed with dismay. Mr. Mortimer, who was not very well at this time, though he concealed his illness from his family, took this unexpected event greatly to heart; within sight of their native land, successful in beating off a French privateer, and now to fall into the power of a ship from which there was no escape. The cup of happiness seemed dashed from their lips, in its stead separation and a dreary imprisonment.

From this despondency our hero strove to rouse them, Annie who was of a hopeful and cheerful temper aiding her lover.

"You will no doubt be immediately exchanged," remarked the young man, "cartels are constantly granted between the two countries, and prisoners are well treated."

Having succeeded in producing some degree of hope in the Mortimer family, he returned to the deck. There all were desponding; all knew captivity and loss of property awaited them.

The huge ship was within two miles of them, when a shot across the fore foot of the Cumberland warned her to lie to.

Our hero gazed sadly at the approaching foe. The wind blew very fresh, and the sea was heavy. It was a grand sight; the great

ship spurning the huge waves, as they rudely
leaped against her monstrous bows, dashing
themselves into wreaths of foam, and scattering their glittering sprays harmlessly over
her lofty decks.

CHAPTER IV.

THE French ship, whose decks were crowded with men, great numbers being soldiers, as soon as she came within two hundred yards of the Cumberland, swung round her immense yards, and lay to, and at once got ready to put down her boats.

This ship was the Droits de l'Homme, the flag-ship of rear Admiral Bouvet, but then commanded by Commodore Le Crosse. She formed one of the fleet of ships intended for the invasion of Ireland; on board was the famous General Humbert.

All on the deck of the Cumberland awaited with intense anxiety the approach of the French boats. They soon came alongside, and two or three officers ascended to the deck, and took possession of her as a prize, ordering the hands to come up from below and assemble on deck, as they were immediately to be removed on board the man-of-war. As one of the French officers turned round, our hero caught sight of his features; he was a very young man scarcely a year older than himself, and extremely good looking; he was attired in a lieutenant's uniform. Walking up to the Frenchman, our hero said, laying his hand on his arm, "Monsieur Pusaye, do you remember me?"

"Ah, parbleu! I do," returned the lieutenant, catching him by the hand, which he pressed kindly, "when last we met I was the prisoner, and you the conqueror; but, never fear, it delights me to be able to return kindness for kindness. Commodore le Crosse, who commands the Droit is my uncle, and he is a kind and considerate commander; he will be pleased to show kindness and attention to one who so essentially served his nephew."

" Then," said our hero, " I will beg your
interference for a family of the name of
Mortimer, passengers on board this ill-starred
ship. Mr. Mortimer is one of the wealthiest
merchants in England, and has his wife,
daughter, infant son, and two female servants
with him."

" *Soyez tranquille, mon ami*," said Lieut.
Pusaye, " I will see to that. Now let us get
them into the long-boat; once on the deck of
the Droits, every attention will be paid
them."

" So far," said our hero, as he turned into
the cabin, " this is a bit of good fortune."

The females were full of anxiety, but
Augustus told them of his fortunate meeting
with an old acquaintance amongst the enemy's
officers. He then wrapped up little Henry
in shawls, and carried him, whilst Annie
grasped his disengaged arm, Mr. Mortimer,
taking care of his beloved wife, they
thus ascended to the deck. The grace and
elegance of Mrs. Mortimer, and the extraordi-

nary beauty of her daughter, instantly attracted the attention of the French officers. Lieut. Pusaye gave orders that any luggage they required, if their servants pointed it out, should be taken on board the Droits. The sea was so rough, that it took more than three hours to transport all on board the Cumberland to the decks of the Droits.

Mrs. Mortimer and her youthful daughter created great interest. Commodore le Crosse, at once ordered them private cabins in the after part of the ship, and begged them to use the state cabin when they pleased. Mr. Mortimer and Captain Inglis were put under the purser's care, Lieut. Pusaye took charge of our hero; and the rest of the prisoners were placed in the cable tier.

A prize master was then sent on board the captured vessel, retaining the chief mate and the cook. The Cumberland was then despatched to seek a French port.

Lieutenant Chamberlain shared the French lieutenant's cabin, and speaking the French language fluently, his situation was far from disagreeable, especially as Commodore le Crosse had assured Mrs. Mortimer that their imprisonment would be short, for, on arriving at Brest, steps would be immediately taken for an exchange of prisoners.

One day, whilst walking the deck with Mrs. Mortimer and daughter, Annie, who was quite resigned and exceedingly cheerful, asked her lover how he came so fortunately to know Lieutenant Pusaye, who was so kind and attentive to them all.

"My previous knowledge of Lieutenant Pusaye has turned out most fortunate, my dearest Annie. About three years ago (I was a midshipman then, and our ship re-fitting in spars in Falmouth), some of the pilots of that port brought in word to Captain Pellew, the commander of a thirty-two gun frigate which was in Falmouth Harbour, that a French frigate was cruising three or four leagues off the Lizard Point. Captain Pellew instantly started in pursuit, and as we were

all idle and the frigate short of hands,
one of our lieutenants, myself, and half a
dozen hands, got leave to go out for a cruise
in search of the French ship."

" How you sailors do love to go where you
risk life," said Annie, looking into her lover's
face with a sweet, half serious, expression on
her countenance.

" Yes, dearest, we do, but we seek, in
risking life, our country's glory and our
own fame. Well, we sailed, and the third
day fell in with a French cruiser, a large,
first class frigate, of more guns and superior
tonnage than ours. Nevertheless, we fought
her for twelve hours, and took her; and it was
allowed by both French and English judges,
one of the most spirited contests on record.
During the boarding, I perceived a young
midshipman, about my own age, knocked
down by a blow from a sailor's cutlass; a
man with a pike was just on the point of
finishing his career, when I ran up, guarded

off the thrust of the pike, and saved the midshipman by making him my prisoner. That midshipman was Lieutenant Pusaye.

"We returned to Falmouth in triumph with our prize, and during a fortnight the young Frenchman remained on board our ship, and soon after we sailed he was exchanged. Captain Pellew now commands the Indefatigable, one of the finest ships in our service."

"We never know, dear Augustus, when a kind, generous act will reap its reward; but tell me why this great ship keeps going in and out of Irish ports; why does she not return to France."

"The fact is, Annie, the great expedition against Ireland must have failed. I only speak from some conversation I hear now and then amongst the officers, who expected to fall in with the fleet that left Brest, which I have no doubt our men-of-war have dispersed, and perhaps captured many vessels.

However, I hear that they intend to-morrow, if none of the ships of their fleet make their appearance, to return to Brest."

The English officer was right respecting the movements of the Droits de l'Homme, the next day she shaped her course across channel for the French coast, intending to make her first land-fall at Belle Isle.

On the 9th they lost sight of the coast of Ireland, and for several days made little progress ; on the 13th Commodore le Crosse considered himself to be about twenty-five leagues from the French coast, and thick, blowing weather coming in, he determined not to approach any nearer; accordingly the Droits stood to the southward, under easy sail, the wind fresh and squally. About noon the next day, a ship was seen to windward, which in the fog loomed very large. She was scarcely a league distant ; almost immediately after a second ship was seen astern of the first. Judging them to be enemies, the Droits immediately prepared for action, and also set more sail, so as to gain time for pre-parations. The wind from the westward increased considerably, and the sea became turbulent. Having run some distance to the south-east, two other ships were discovered, endeavouring to cut off the French vessel from the land.

By this time the two ships first seen had come near enough to distinguish them clearly. Lieutenant Pusaye was regarding them with his glass, our hero standing close beside him.

"They are English," said the French lieutenant, handing Chamberlain the glass, "perhaps you may recognize them. The nearest is a very large frigate."

Our hero, after a steady look, returned the glass, saying,

"Yes, I recognize the nearest ship. It is the "Indefatigable," a forty-four gun frigate, and commanded by one of the finest fellows in our navy. You may remember Captain Pellew, who commanded the Nymph in her spirited action with the Cleopatra."

" Ah, sacre bleu ! I ought to remember it well," returned the lieutenant, " but surely the frigate will scarcely run the terrible risk of encountering a seventy-four gun ship, and her consort more than a league astern."

Our hero smiled, saying, " We shall see."

" If she does," said Lieutenant Pusaye, " you surely need not run the risk of being shot down by your countrymen's fire."

" If I am permitted," said our hero, " I will remain on deck."

Whilst yet speaking, a sudden and tremendous squall struck the huge ship, carried away the main-top braces, and at the same time her fore and main top-masts. All for the moment became confusion : the sea was so rough that the lower deck ports were shut, whilst the ship was going through the water about six knots under her courses and mizen topsail.

The Indefatigable was full eight miles ahead of her consort, a thirty-six gun frigate, called the Amazon.

The English frigate, to the great amazement of the officers of the Droits, hauled up to pour in a raking fire, but the Droits hauled up also, discharged her broadside, and poured in a tremendous fire of musketry from the troops on board. The Indefatigable then tried to pass ahead, but the enemy defeated that manœuvre, and attempted to storm the deck of the frigate, but this intent was skilfully avoided by the British commander. The violence of the sea had rendered her broadside comparatively harmless.

For two hours a spirited fight was maintained between the two ill-matched combatants, till, about six o'clock p.m., the Amazon came up under a press of sail and poured her broadside into the seventy-four, at scarcely pistol-shot distance.

The incidents of our tale will not permit us to dwell upon the particulars of this most extraordinary conflict between the two frigates and the French ship. One on each side of the Droits, they kept up an incessant fire, a tremendous gale continuing the entire time.

The Droits having expended all her round shot, began firing shells ; many of the crew were slain, but not till the morning of the 14th were any of the officers wounded, when a grape shot struck the arm of one of the lieutenants, and Lieut. Pusaye, beside whom our hero was standing watching this strange and furious contest, was struck down by a splinter. He was raised to be taken below ; but he had been only stunned for a moment, and refused to leave the deck.

During the whole of this action, the sea ran so high that the crew and people on the main deck of the frigates, were up to their middles in water,° and so violent was the motion of the ships, that the guns of the Indefatigable drew out the ring-bolts; she had also four feet of water in the hold. Worn out with fatigue, the crews of all the ships ceased from their

* James's Naval History,

fourteen hours' contention. More terrible
perils awaited them.

Mrs. Mortimer and family remained in sus-
pense and terror, confined to their couches
from the terrible rolling and plunging of the
almost ungovernable ship.

"Thank God," said the mother to her
daughter, "this horrible firing has ceased at
last, and my poor terrified boy sleeps."

"Ah, poor Harry, what a trial for so young
a child," said Annie trembling. Her heart and
thoughts were with Augustus, for well she
knew he would keep the deck. Mrs. Mortimer was aware that her husband was not exposed to the firing, for our hero wrote a few
lines on a slip of paper, and Lieutenant
Pusaye got it conveyed to the terrified wife.
Alas, how little they thought of the terrible
enemy they were too soon to contend with.

About four o'clock a.m., of the fourteenth,
the moon suddenly shone forth from amid
the storm-tossed clouds. With a cry of horror
several of the crew shouted "Land! Land,

right ahead!" This cry struck a chill to the hearts of all that heard it.

Lieutenant Chamberlain was holding on, and gazing anxiously at the Indefatigable, which was then close to the Droits' starboard, and the Amazon near on the larboard.

The British frigate must have seen the land at the same time, for instantly the crew hauled on board the tacks, and made sail to the southward; the Amazon unfortunately bore to the northward.

"Gallantly and bravely done," exclaimed our hero enthusiastically, as he beheld the noble ship respond to the cool efforts of her crew, and turned on the foaming deep, dashing the wild waves, as if in scorn, from her bows though buried in a world of waters. She still answered her helm, and stood triumphantly out of the awful peril, that, ten minutes later, overwhelmed her consort and the ill-fated Droits de l'Homme.

Utterly helpless, the ragged main-sail dragging through the wild seas, the foremast and bowsprit, falling over the bows, there was nothing left but to let go the anchors; but all the anchors except two had been lost in Bantry Bay, and the cables had been cut through by the shot of the enemy. Two anchors however, were let go, in twelve fathoms water, but they did not hold for an instant, and on went the doomed ship to her grave. Five minutes of horror, and she struck, with a terrible shock ; at the second shock her mainmast went by the board.

The French sailors, in their terrible situation had still the gallantry and courage of their nation in their hearts. They rushed to the hatchways, calling out, in loud voices, " Pauvre Anglais! Come up on deck, quick; we are all lost."

Our hero well knew that no effort of man could save the ship, and all restraint being now at an end, he and the distracted Mr. Mortimer hurried to join his wife and family. Mrs. Mortimer, with her boy clasped to her heart, rushed to meet her husband. Our hero clasped the hand of his betrothed; she was firm and calm.

"Do not give way to despair, dear Mrs. Mortimer," said our hero, "every effort will be made, and, depend on it, the French seamen are as gallant and as anxious to save the lives of the females, as any other nation under the sun; so, dear lady, keep up your spirit and heart, this ship will not break up for days, at all events, and the gale is sure to moderate to-night, or indeed at any moment."

"You inspire me with hope, dear Augustus," replied Mrs. Mortimer, kissing the fair forehead of her sleeping boy, whilst a tear fell on its little face. "God is merciful," she continued, "I do not dread death myself, but these dear young souls, only springing into life, to be crushed in the bud; alas! alas!" and she bent her head to hide the tears that would flow.

Mr. Mortimer was not of a sanguine disposition; he looked sad and disturbed, but joined in the words of hope spoken by the English sailor. As to Annie Mortimer, she gazed fondly into her lover's hopeful countenance, pressed his hand, as he was departing, and whispered to him, with a look that sunk into his heart, "Remember, we live or die together."

"Live, beloved, is my hope," returned the youth; "but if death it is to be, it shall be as you say, together."

Meanwhile, the vessel swayed backwards and forwards fearfully with each blow she received from the huge rollers that dashed with relentless force against her sides, deluging the deck, and dashing the helpless soldiers and women about the deck, and even washing some of them overboard. All hands were heaving the guns into the sea, in order if possible to keep her upright. Just opposite the little village of Audierne— for on a bank that crossed that bay the Droits de l'Homme lay—amidst the spray raised by the breakers, could now and then be seen the hull of the unfortunate Amazon, over which the wild waves broke with awful force. It was, in truth, an awful sight which the deck of the doomed Droits presented to the gaze of our hero. Even the seas that washed over her had not cleared away the traces and marks of the sanguinary combat so fatally interrupted; not a mast was standing, whilst a crowd of unmanageable and terrified soldiers, driven here and there, and knocked down by the shocks the ship received from the seas—some, in stupified groups—were clinging to any object they could grasp.

As night came on the remorseless sea increased in fury, and, as the tide again rose, the rollers came thundering against the lofty sides of the ship, glorying in their might, and hurrying to destruction their disabled victim. All distinction of rank, all attempts at discipline, became submerged in the one feeling—dear life. Commodore le Crosse and General Humbert, however, did all they could to pro-

tect the ladies, and had a place barricaded
and filled with mattresses to enable them to
bear the terrible shocks the vessel received as
the tide came to its height.

An awful night was passed, in hourly
expectation of the ship's parting asunder.
During the darkness numbers perished—swept
off the decks by the raging sea. The next
day the shore could be seen, lined with people,
but, in the fearful gale still raging, no assistance could be rendered.   As soon as it was
low water some of the boats were launched,
the first two were dashed to pieces before a
soul could enter them.   A pass-rope was
tried, and then a raft, which was made fast
and slacked by degrees from the ship to permit it to drift ashore ; but the furious seas
washed some off, and then the rest cut the
rope, and the raft, with some eight or ten,
reached the shore.

After various and many failures, the day
closed, and another awful night ensued. The
stern was stove in and filled the cabin with water.

All on board had now been thirty hours without food. On the third day the captain and English seamen, formerly the crew of the Cumberland, came to our hero, and told him they were going to attempt to make land in a small boat, and wanted him to join them and steer; they felt confident that they would succeed at low water in reaching the shore. "Frenchmen," said Captain Inglis, "are bad managers of small boats."

At this time it was very evident that in another day, exposed and half-starved as all were, Mrs. Mortimer and the baby would succumb to their trials. Mr. Mortimer laboured under affliction of body, as well as mind. Annie, during the long and terrible night, was supported by the arms of her betrothed, and any food and wine he procured by immense exertions on his part, was divided between the baby and Annie. She did not know that he had not tasted food himself for thirty hours.

In reply to the English sailor's request, Augustus Chamberlain said—

"As to me I cannot accept your offer, but take in my place Mrs. Mortimer and her child."

"Most willingly," exclaimed the men, "make haste and prepare her, and, please God, we will make the shore."

Our hero hurried to the place of shelter, if shelter it could now be called, where the females crouched together, sobbing and lamenting their sad fate. When he named the plan of relief, and hope of safety, father and mother shuddered—but our hero felt so confident of the skill of the crew of the Cumberland, that Mrs. Mortimer said—

"For the sake of this dear babe I will go; live till to-morrow here, we cannot."

Mr. Mortimer himself feebly consented, and after a heart-rending embrace of husband and child, the mother and her baby, wrapped closely in shawls, were conducted by our hero on deck. For a moment Mrs. Mortimer became bewildered by the sight of horror the deck presented. At this time three hundred of the souls aboard the ship had perished. Not a single Frenchman would attempt a landing in so small a boat—it was certain death they said—Alas! was not death already busy aboard.

"Go, Mr. Chamberlain," said one of the English crew ; "go with the lady, and I will stay here and take my chance."

"No, my gallant fellow," said our hero, "I have a task to accomplish, or perish."

"Then, blow me," said Tom Darking, the name of the sailor, a great favourite of our hero, when on board the Cumberland, "if I don't stay and help you; the boat will be lighter and better without me. There will be four of us left to assist you to get Miss Mortimer safe ashore."

Our hero pressed the young man's hand firmly, saying "Those words shall not be forgotten if Providence enables us to get out of this doomed ship to the shore."

The boat was carefully launched, and Mrs. Mortimer safely placed with her darling boy in

E 5

the stern sheets. As the frail barque shoved off, even amid their sufferings, a cheer from all who beheld the departure mingled with the howl of the pitiless wind.

"Mon Dieu!" said Captain Le Crosse, who just then came up "that boat will never reach the shore with that unfortunate lady and child."

Looking up into the Frenchman's face, the expression of which was sad and solemn, our hero said, "with God's help it will; I am confident of the skill and courage of the men who man that boat; besides," he added, in a voice trembling with emotion, "another night and the mother and child would cease to exist."

"Alas!" said the commodore "you are right, we are in the hands of God. If this gale lasts thirty hours longer, few will remain alive, to tell the tale of our disaster."

All watched the little craft, almost unconscious of their own sufferings, so intense was their anxiety for the gallant souls in the little boat. Over the huge waves it rose, at times

hid by showers of spray, then down into the
gulf between the seas, then again skilfully
handled, it rose to view, and presently
plunged into the rollers, and one huge one
caught it, lifted it aloft, and then, with the
speed of the racehorse, it rushed upon the
rocks, but numbers were already in the sea
to receive and save the living freight, and before the boat struck, all had been seized, and
carried ashore.

"Grace à dieu!" cried Lieutenant Pusaye,
looking at those on the shore with his glass
"they are all saved, and now, Monsieur
Chamberlain, what will you do for her who
is dearer to you than life?"

The young man started, but immediately
said, "I will attempt to save her and her
father on a raft. It is too late to-day; if God
spares us another, it must be tried."

"Yes," observed the French lieutenant,
"You are right, delay is death, this fearful
gale has a dozen lives."

Augustus Chamberlain then held a consul-

tation with the sailor Tom Darking, a fine,
high-spirited, athletic young fellow, who
said that he and his four comrades of the
Cumberland could construct a raft, lashing
empty barrels to the sides, and carrying sail,
that should take them to the land safely.

"These Frenchmen, your honour," said
Tom, "are brave, kind fellows, and fight till
all's blue, and die plucky, but they are no
hands in small boats; once wrecked they are
done for, they become helpless."

"Well, Tom, get all ready, and, please God,
if we survive the night, we'll push off for the
shore."

Notwithstanding every exertion on the
part of our hero, and the heroic self denial
of Annie Mortimer, who, in concealing her
own great sufferings, sought to cheer the
terrible despondency of Mr. Mortimer, all
was vain They did not know that Mr.
Mortimer suffered from disease of the heart,
which had become greatly aggravated by
their misfortunes in being captured by the

Droits, followed by the disastrous shipwreck. Our hero assured him of his wife's and child's safety, for which he thanked God fervently.

"Still," said Mr. Mortimer, "look at the state to which we are reduced; we cannot last another night and day without food or drink. You have given the last drop of wine, denying yourself, to Annie, and she, poor child, insisted on giving it to me, for she feared I was sinking."

"Be of good heart, sir," said the young lieutenant, "I have a raft constructing, and a few gallant hearts to man it. These Frenchmen, half dead as they are, will not peril the little life they have left upon a raft; the fate of those who embarked on the two last has terrified all."

That night the storm increased in violence; and the unfortunate beings on the wreck were momentarily perishing. Commodore Le Crosse secretly gave our hero a bottle of wine, one of the last he possessed, to support Miss Mortimer and the other females, in the place of shelter they still retained. How fervently they blessed the noble hearted youth, who served each of them with a glass, thinking nothing of himself. Annie with the tears running down her wasted cheeks, implored him to take even half a glass. But he laughed cheerfully, saying "he did not need it, he was strong enough, and had had a good draught of water."

Alas! that was not truth, for water at this time it was impossible to have. But during the night it rained, and water was caught, which saved many from madness.

Two hours after day-break, the gale still blowing furiously, Tom Darking announced that the raft was ready. The huge seas flew furiously over the vessel, shaking her to her keelson. Our hero tried to persuade one or two of the females to come with them; they shuddered at the idea ; none had the courage to brave instant death for the chance of life.

" You are not afraid, my beloved," said our hero, to the sweet, fair, faded girl he almost carried in his arms, whilst Tom Darking supported Mr. Mortimer.

"Afraid," answered Annie, "oh, no. Not afraid, whilst with you."

The kind-hearted Frenchmen did all they could to assist the brave Anglais. "You are going to certain death," they said, "the first sea after you clear the ship will wash you all off."

The four sailors got on the raft, the ropes held by some of the French crew. With considerable care and great attention, Augustus Chamberlain, supporting Annie in his arms was lowered on to the raft—a work of great difficulty, Tom Darking staying to assist Mr. Mortimer who was in a kind of stupor. At that moment an enormous roller came suddenly upon the ship; it reared its great crested head, and broke with a hideous roar against the side of the seventy-four, sweeping many of the men into the surge, breaking the rope of the raft, and sending the raft itself fifty yards from the ship; but not before Tom Darking, quick as thought, threw himself on to the raft, just as it rose and dashed from the ship.

A cry of intense agony escaped Annie Mortimer's lips. She just knew that her beloved father was left behind, and then she fainted—completely overcome.

Back no human power could take them; that morning there was a slight shift of wind, which would, if the raft survived the shocks of the seas, in passing over the bank, take them some distance up the bay, by which circumstance they would avoid the dangerous reefs of rocks that lined the shore by Audierne.

Lashing Annie carefully to the middle of the raft, and seizing the great spar, Tom had lashed to one end of the raft to steer by, our hero guided the wildly-tossed raft, whilst the five men hoisted a lug sail. This sail preserved them—each having also a rope's end, to secure himself from being washed off. After clearing the ship the sea broke furiously

over them; but the raft, under her sail, drove
before the gale, and, by superhuman exertions,
they carried her through the great rollers on
the bank, and getting into deeper water, the
regular sea was then more easily encountered.
Leaving Tom to steer, our hero took his
affianced's head upon his knee, pushed back
her long tresses of rich auburn hair, and
gazed anxiously and earnestly into her death-
like features. The poor drenched and worn-
out maiden opened her eyes—her first words
were, " Oh, my father! my father! we have
left him to perish."

Just then one of the men called out " A sail.
A sail to windward of the seventy-four standing towards her."

Augustus looked round, and saw a large
vessel, judging by the loftiness of her topsail,
standing into the bay.

" Look, dearest," and he raised the young
girl, till her eyes rested on the distant sail.
" That ship will anchor near the wreck, and
before to-morrow your father will be saved."

Annie gave a sigh of relief; the poor girl was nearly exhausted.

"Now, sir," shouted Tom Darking, "We are getting quite close to the breakers."

Augustus saw clearly that there would be a desperate struggle to undergo in passing through the breaking seas that thundered down upon the beach. All objects on the shore were hidden by the clouds of spray from the crests of the surges, as they raced madly towards the beach.

Augustus's first care was to unloose the young girl from the cords that had saved her from being washed off. He had a strong leather belt round his own waist.

"Now, dearest, grasp this belt firmly; when the raft strikes we shall, no doubt, be thrown off. Yet do not give way to fear. I will, with God's blessing, bear you to the shore."

The roller came high over them — it towered. Annie closed her eyes, and grasped the belt, whilst our hero, encircling her with

his strong arm, awaited the struggle for life.
The roller came on, dashed pitilessly upon
the frail craft, and swept everyone upon it
into the boiling surf.

A bold swimmer, and of wonderful power
of endurance, Augustus sustained his helpless
burden. Keeping her head above water, and
letting the next roller drive them on to the
beach, and then, exerting his last remnant of
strength, he bore her up out of reach of the
next sea, and then sank down beside her,
nearly overcome.

It was quite true that the sail those on the
raft saw was the sail of a man-of-war brig,
called the Arrogant. This vessel, and a
cutter, called the Aiguille, both French,
stood as far into the bay as safety warranted,
and then anchored. As soon as possible, they
hoisted out their boats, and courageously
pulled through the breaking seas to the
wreck. By this time it was almost night·
Nevertheless, eager to assist those still on
board the wreck, they eagerly prepared a

large raft, and before night one hundred and fifty, out of nearly four hundred who still remained on board, were safe in the brig. Night, and a return of the gale, forced the boats to discontinue; but the next morning the wind suddenly lulled, and the boats put off. But, alas! during the long hours of the night, nearly two hundred had perished, one way or another, amongst them the unfortunate Mr. Mortimer, whose sufferings of mind and body left him incapable of sustaining another night of agony; and though Commodore Le Crosse had his body taken on board the cutter, no remedies applied could restore life.

General Humbert and a Lieutenant Pipon were saved, and, with the captain of the ship, were taken to the cutter, which got immediately under weigh, and proceeded to Brest. There Mr. Mortimer was decently buried, by order of the commodore. Messengers were sent also by his directions to Audierne, to bring Mrs. Mortimer and infant

and daughter, if saved, to Brest; but the
awful calamity that had fallen on the Mortimer family by the capture of the Cumberland
was only to end in death of father, mother,
and infant. Though saved and carried to
Audierne, and treated kindly by the people of
the place, the poor boy had gone through
too much suffering to live, and sank to rest
in his mother's arms the second day after
leaving the wreck. The distraction of the
mother was pitiable; her distress being
aggravated by the French authorities sending
a party of soldiers to take all the English
saved from the wreck to Quimper. There
the unfortunate lady was attacked by fever,
and though treated kindly, and some English
females, also prisoners, allowed to attend on
her, she gradually sank, and, murmuring the
name of her husband, her adored boy, and
daughter, she ceased to exist. In the parish
churchyard of St. Etienne was Mrs. Mortimer
buried, and a few days after, two other females,
who also owed their death to their suffer-

ings on board the doomed seventy-four. The
remainder of the English prisoners, along
with the officers and crew of the Amazon,
were sent on to Brest; and the French
government, in consideration of their sufferings, and the help they had given to save the
lives of the people cast ashore from the Droits
de l'Homme, granted them a cartel, and,
finally, in the month of March, they were all
landed in Plymouth, without exchange or
ransom.

CHAPTER IV.

THE non-arrival of the Cumberland Packet
in England some weeks after the time of its
expected appearance had elapsed, caused great
anxiety and uneasiness to many besides her
owners.   Mr. Mortimer and family were
known to have embarked, for a Government
vessel had touched at Barbadoes three days
after the departure of the Cumberland, and
brought home, besides other particulars, a list
of the passengers.

In a handsome house in Cavendish Square
resided a gentleman of the name of Calthurst,
a solicitor of high character, good standing,
great practice, and experience.   He was Mr.

Mortimer's agent and solicitor, and had the entire control of his accumulated wealth. Some months previous to the opening chapter of our tale, he had made a most advantageous purchase of a fine mansion and estate, called St. Quentin, within six miles of Christchurch; and situated on the sea coast. This estate he had purchased for £85,000. The house attached had only been built a few years, and was considered remarkably handsome, both as regarded its exterior appearance, and the beauty of the grounds surrounding it. Mr. Calthurst had also received the purchase-money of the Barbadoes estate, and had it safely invested till Mr. Mortimer's return to England. As everything was prepared at St. Quentin for the immediate reception of the family when they should arrive, Mr. Calthurst and his family (consisting of his wife, one son, and two daughters), became every day more anxious concerning the arrival of the Cumberland Packet.

But when three weeks had passed beyond

the naturally expected time of her arrival, their anxiety became exchanged for alarm. Mr. Calthurst came home one day to his dinner very late; his family were waiting for him, and his agitated manner as he entered the drawing-room at once attracted their attention.

"No bad news, father, I hope," said his son John (a youth of twenty-two), "of the expected packet?"

"I deeply regret to say," returned the father, "that there are very ugly and serious rumours afloat at Lloyd's. It is reported, indeed, positively asserted, that the Cumberland Packet has been captured by some French vessel-of-war."

"Good heavens! how unfortunate," exclaimed mother and daughters. "But who could bring such intelligence?"

"Better that, however," said the son, "than being lost at sea. But who spread such a report, sir?"

"A schooner from Cadiz bound to Falmouth," said Mr. Calthurst. "Her captain stated to Lloyd's agent there, that on the first of January he spoke the Cumberland Packet, then like himself working to windward—that night a thick fog and heavy weather separated them ; but on the third, when the fog cleared, he was then on the starboard tack, the coast of Ireland in sight, and he saw through his glass the Cumberland lying-to, and close to her also a 74 or 90-gun ship, with French colours flying—that he at once slacked his sheets, and made for the mouth of the Shannon, and anchored—that continual bad weather kept him there nearly three weeks. At Lloyd's this account is believed to be true."

The servant announcing dinner, the family proceeded to the dining parlour. During the repast the conversation continually reverted to the Mortimers.

Suddenly John Calthurst laid aside his knife and fork, saying, " By-the-by, father, who would succeed to the Mortimer property, should any fatality overwhelm the whole family ?"

"Who," said the father, looking up into his son's face with a very serious expression, "a person *you* know very well, John, and against whose acquaintance, beyond mere civility, I have often cautioned you. I mean Mr. Herbert Delme ; he, by law, is the next heir, but he is a notorious profligate, a gambler, and a spendthrift—a man without a shilling."

John Calthurst coloured a little, but he immediately said, "Why, sir, you know I cannot, in the way of business, avoid speaking to Mr. Herbert Delme ; he calls here constantly, enquiring after the Mortimers, and besides my sister Bella was introduced to him at Mr. Gardener's party, and I think, Bella, you said you thought him a very agreeable partner, and a very handsome man."

Bella Calthurst had a deeper colour on her pretty fair cheek than her brother, as she said, "Surely Mrs. Gardener ought not to have introduced Mr. Delme to me if he bears such a character as papa gives him."

The dessert was on the table, and the servant had retired, when Mr. Calthurst said, "Mr. Delme's character is not generally known in such circles as we move in. Besides, he is a client of Mr. Gardener's."

"But, John," interrupted Mrs. Calthurst, turning to her husband. "How is Mr. Herbert Delme the next heir to Mr. Mortimer's property?"

"He is only heir to his property," replied Mr. Calthurst, "in case of the death of the whole family — father, mother, son and daughter—which I sincerely trust is not at all probable. If they are prisoners, all they will have to suffer is captivity; they will be exchanged or ransomed. What put such an idea in John's head I cannot imagine."

"It was only a sudden thought," said the son, helping himself to wine; "but now I have started the subject, do tell me, father, something about this Mr. Herbert Delme, for certainly he is a very fashionable young man, mixes in aristocratic society, drives and rides good horses, and seems always flush of cash, and is, they say, next heir to a baronetcy."

"His gold is gained one day at the gaming table," said Mr. Calthurst, " lost the next at the same place. Plunged head and ears in debt; he is left at liberty because his creditors know he is not worth a shilling."

"Good gracious!" said Mrs. Calthurst, laughing. "How silly of them to trust a man they know to be worth a nothing."

"At times he possesses large sums, and he spends them freely ; he boasts of be-ing the only nephew of Mr. Mortimer, who is known to be worth half a million, and that relationship goes a long way with his creditors."

"Well, really," said Mrs. Calthurst, "I did not know he was Mr. Mortimer's nephew, though I knew he was a relation. Mr. Mor-timer had no brother."

"No," said Mr. Calthurst, "but he had a

sister. I have never touched upon, or spoken before you, or any of my family, upon the subject of the Mortimer family. I saw no need of it. Now that, unhappily, there is this strange rumour afloat of even a worse calamity than captivity, I will make you acquainted with a very short family history."

" But what calamity do you speak of worse than captivity?" anxiously enquired mother and daughters.

" I will tell you. It is reported that the Indefatigable, a frigate commanded by Captain Pellew, arrived in Plymouth, greatly cut up from an engagement with a French 74-gun ship, the Droits de l'Homme. She had with her as consort the Amazon frigate; that, after a furious engagement of two days, the Droits de l'Homme and the Amazon were driven ashore on the French coast, and totally wrecked. The Indefatigable, by a miracle, avoided the same fate, and, almost in a sinking condition, managed to make Plymouth. Now, although this 74-gun ship might have been the seventy-four that took the Packet, there is nothing positive in it, except that the dates correspond. Still, even supposing the report true, it does not follow that the Mortimers were on board ; they might have remained prisoners in the Cumberland, and the prize might have made a safe port. Besides, though the seventy-four was driven ashore, a huge ship like that would not break up like a coaster—therefore there is every probability of some of them being saved, for surely all could not perish."

John Calthurst, the son, looked exceedingly thoughtful as he said, seeing his mother and sisters retiring, " You have not told us, sir, how the Mortimer family --"

" Oh!" interrupted Mr. Calthurst, " I forgot. I am so very concerned and anxious about my old friend and his family, and so perplexed by this disastrous intelligence, that I scarcely know what to think or do."

" Well, my dear," said Mrs. Calthurst, " I do not see that you can do anything; a few

days may enlighten us on this subject. If Mr.
Mortimer and family should most unfortunately have perished, it will be a very grand
thing for Mr. Herbert Delme. I will leave
you now to tell John the Mortimer history, as
we are going to a quiet party at the Gardeners'
to-night, and must go and dress, for we have
dined very late."

Mr. Calthurst looked after the showy figure
of his better half with rather a puzzled look.
They were a very attached couple, notwithstanding that their views and intentions were
widely different; but our story will explain
and disclose the various views and projects of
the Calthurst family. We must except,
however, the worthy Mr. Calthurst himself,
who never entertained but one view or project
in his whole life, and that was to rise in the
world by honest industry, and by acting, in
every case and sense, with the strictest inte-
grity.

"Well, sir," said the son, pushing the
decanter over to his father, who seemed

plunged in thought, " I am waiting for your promised account of how Mr. Herbert Delme becomes the next heir to Mr. Mortimer's entire property ? "

" He will never inherit the wealth left by Mr. Mortimer, if, which God forbid, the family have perished," said Mr. Calthurst, emphatically, " let that be sufficient for you to know. I will just, in a few words, give you the private history of my old friend, whom, I trust in God, still lives.

" Mr. Mortimer's father was a very wealthy merchant. He owned large estates in Barbadoes, and when he died left the entire of his wealth, excepting twenty thousand pounds, to his only son, Henry. The twenty thousand pounds were bequeathed to his only daughter, Maria; and in his will he distinctly stated, that if she married against the consent of her brother she should forfeit the twenty thousand pounds, which would then revert to Henry Mortimer. Mr. Mortimer continued the mercantile pursuits; but, four years after

her father's death, Miss Mortimer fell in love
with the then notorious Adolphus Herbert
Delme, the father of the present Herbert
your friend.

"Mr. Adolphus Delme could boast of his
high descent and aristocratic connections, but
there ended his qualifications, if we except a
very handsome person and most insinuating
manners, especially with women. Before he
had reached his thirtieth year he had run
through a fortune of nearly eighty thousand
pounds, became in debt for half that sum, had
fought a dozen duels, killed two of his ill-
starred adversaries, and wounded others. He
was a dreaded man, for he was a dead shot,
a most practiced and skilful swordsman, and
never forgave the slightest provocation. Mr.
Delme secretly gained the love of Miss Mortimer, privately married her, and then, without his wife's knowledge, sought out an
opportunity to be publicly rude to Mr.
Mortimer, who had not the most remote idea
that the man who had so grossly insulted him

was his sister's husband. Duelling was then,* even more than now, the curse of society. Mr. Delme knew that he would never be able to procure Mr. Mortimer's consent to his marriage with his sister, and he actually conceived the horrible design of provoking his brother-in-law into a duel, in order to get quit of him. Mr. Mortimer dead, his wife would inherit her brother's wealth; for Mr. Mortimer, though engaged, was then unmarried. Though detesting duelling, Mr. Mortimer was obliged to give way to the customs and usages of society. He had the choice of weapons, and he chose the small sword, then worn by all gentlemen. He sent for me. I was an old college friend of his, and some four years his senior. I was then just commencing my profession. So sincerely did Mr. Mortimer love his sister, and so little did he suspect his confidence in her abused, that he made a will entirely in her favour, should

* About the year 1770

he fall in his contest with Mr. Delme. I was
sorely troubled and grieved. I knew it was quite
useless to try and prevail on my friend to de-
cline the fighting ; who though a most amiable
and quiet man in all his pursuits, had a
high and haughty spirit. A blow in the face,
before the members of the club to which he
and Mr. Delme both belonged, was not to be
borne with impunity.

Well, to shorten my tale, and a sad tale
it is—and it strongly points out that man
may plan and devise, but God directs, that
the race is not always to the swift, or the
battle to the strong—strange to say, without
any particular skill in his weapon, whilst his
adversary was renowned for his consummate
dexterity, Mr. Mortimer ran Mr. Delme through
the body the very third pass made between
them ; the seconds on both sides stood confounded—this was a result none expected.
Adolphus Herbert Delme was, however, mortally wounded. Struck with remorse, he
implored Mr. Mortimer's forgiveness, stated

that he was his sister's husband, and that he
had purposely provoked the duel that so
terribly ended his career.

"Mr. Mortimer was horrified, shocked, and
distracted; he had killed his sister's husband,
though certainly without knowing him to be
such; the idea was overpowering, and the
next day he was in a high fever.   Three
months elapsed before he recovered his mind
and health.   During that time his sister had
given birth to the present Mr. Delme, and
died.

"I shall not attempt to describe or to
analyze Mr. Mortimer's feelings—sufficient to
say he sometime after married, and at once embarked for Barbadoes, leaving his sister's child
under the care of guardians, and settling upon
him a sum of forty thousand pounds. I declined
to be one of the guardians.   I had my own
reasons for so doing, and Mr. Mortimer did
not attempt to refute them.   When Mr.
Herbert Delme became of age he consequently
succeeded to the forty thousand pounds and

the accumulated amount of interest, made the most of during a long minority. His guardians, I must say, did their duty with the money entrusted to their care; but they had not troubled themselves much how the young man was brought up. He went to Harrow and to Oxford, certainly; but he only brought away the vices, and none of the learning or accomplishments to be gained in those places.

" The career of Mr. Herbert Delme I need not paint to you—you have heard enough of it   It will be quite sufficient to say that in six or seven years after getting possession of his noble fortune he was without a shilling, and, like his father, over head and ears in debt. Mr. Mortimer was quite aware of the career his nephew was running, and at first tried, by all the means in his power, to check it; but only received vain promises of reform, till, disgusted, he left him to pursue a course that has finished by making him the most unprincipled profligate in this great city.

" Now let us go up, and get a cup of tea—
this re-calling of the past has been painful to
me; but I hope you may profit by it."

Whilst Mr. Calthurst was relating the
history just recorded, in the dining room, his
wife and her two daughters were partaking of
a cup of coffee or tea in the drawing room,
previous to retiring to dress.

The two Miss Calthursts were really fine,
showy girls, and quite conscious that
they were so. Bella, the youngest, then
eighteen, was generally admitted to be a
very handsome girl. She had brilliant
dark eyes and hair, a beautiful complexion, and a very elegant figure—the only
drawback was a " *nez retroussé;*" but some
admired this sort of feature. Be it as it may,
it certainly became her.

The elder sister was nearly twenty—tall
and well-made—a blonde, and with better
features altogether than her sister; but was
not, by any means, so much admired. They
were both accomplished girls, and might, but

for one fault, have made excellent wives, if they had had the good fortune to have looked for husbands in their own sphere of life; but their whole thoughts and ideas, encouraged by their ambitious mother, was to marry out of their own station in society. Thus their otherwise amiable dispositions became wrecked upon the rock of ambition.

Now, though Mr. Herbert Delme was not worth, as Mr. Calthurst said, a single shilling, he was, nevertheless, heir to a barren baronetcy, and that was something in the eyes of the world. Sir Edgar Hopeton Delme was the last, if we except Mr. Herbert Delme, of the male descendants of a once high and opulent family. He had lived a life of wild extravagance in continental cities, and, at the age of eighty-four, was existing on a small annuity bestowed upon him by an old friend, to keep him from the sufferings of real poverty. So, as far as the title went, Mr. Herbert Delme could boast of being the probable successor in a very short period, for Sir

Edgar could not live through the winter, his doctor said.

Mrs. Calthurst, as she poured out the tea and coffee, said to her daughters, " This is a very sudden calamity—this loss of Mr. Mortimer's family—for I cannot divest my mind of the idea but that they are all lost. It's very terrible to think of such a catastrophe as a whole family, and possessed of such wealth, perishing, as you may say, within sight of their native shores."

" It is indeed fearful, mamma," said Bella, " quite shocking. They must have suffered so much, too, when they were taken by the French ship-of-war."

" I think it quite possible," said the elder sister, " that one out of the four may have been saved."

" It's very possible," said Mrs. Calthurst; " still, in my opinion, Mr. Delme has every chance of succeeding to an immense fortune. Mrs. Gardener says his follies and extravagance are greatly magnified—he is not a quarter so bad as report represents him to be. I daresay we shall see him to-night. He is usually very attentive to you, Bella."

" Oh, I think him very agreeable, and certainly he is very handsome," replied Bella.

" When a man marries, and he likes his wife," said Mrs. Calthurst, " he soon determines to lead a steadier life."

" You may depend on it, mother," said the eldest Miss Calthurst, " once this intelligence of the Mortimers' melancholy fate gets abroad, and is positively verified, and Mr. Delme steps into the shoes of the old baronet, his youthful follies will be styled—exuberance of spirit and thoughtlessness, and a too generous disposition—he will have plenty of admirers amongst our sex."

" Such is my opinion," answered Mrs. Calthurst, " and I tell you what, Mrs. Gardener told me in confidence that Bella had made a great impression on Mr. Delme; and, although Sir Edgar Delme is living on a small annuity, the moment he died, an estate in Somersetshire, worth more than two thousand a-year, would be liable to dispute ; and if Mr. Delme had funds to carry on the lawsuit that estate, at all events, would be his. But come, we must go and dress. By the way, if this intelligence is positively true, it would be very wrong for us to go out this evening ; but as it is a mere rumour, of course there is no impropriety in our going to a quiet party."

" I should think not," said Miss Calthurst, who expected to meet the Honourable William Hall Pemberton, a gentleman client of Mr. Gardener, who was trying to borrow some twenty thousand pounds, upon very scanty security, and who would have had no objection to a plebeian wife with that amount of incumbrance.

Mr. Calthurst's office, where his six clerks worked from nine o'clock a.m. to five p.m. was in Welbeck-street; there he had also his own private sitting room and office in which to receive his clients.

His son John was about to be taken into

partnership. Mr. Calthurst had amassed a very fine fortune—he could give each of his two daughters during his life six thousand pounds, with a prospect of having as much more at his death.

About one o'clock in the day on the following morning, Mr. John Calthurst, junior, was sitting in his father's office, reading the Times, or imagining that he was reading that broad sheet; but, in point of fact, he was thinking of matters very irrelevant to newspaper intelligence. He had been engaged the preceding evening, and therefore did not accompany his mother and sisters to Mr. Gardener's. One of the clerks entered the room, saying, " Mr. Delme wishes to see you, Mr. John. He first enquired for your father. I told him your father was engaged in the city. He then asked for you, saying you would do as well. Shall I show him in ? "

"Certainly, Gilmore—shew him in ; I cannot refuse to see Mr. Delme."

In less than five minutes that gentleman

entered the office; he immediately turned round, and looked steadfastly at the clerk, who, bowing and somewhat discomposed, closed the door as he retired.

"Ah!" said Mr. Delme, with a light laugh, "a discreet young man. Well, John, how goes it," holding out his hand. "Rum is riz, and sugars is fell, as they say east of Temple Bar, eh, John, what do you think?"

"Well, upon my faith I do not know what to think, Herbert. I know I lost seventy odd pounds last night, and that my exchequer is at low tide."

"Never mind, my lad; the 'jade fortune' is as fickle as—what the deuce shall I say;— I'm sick of quoting women; but, look here." And he took a roll of notes out of his pocket as he threw himself into a chair. "After you left I made a splendid haul. There is a cool hundred for you to commence business with to-morrow night. When one's up, the other's down. There, pocket these," and he coolly tossed John Calthurst two fifty-pound notes, which the young man quietly accepted, saying—

" What's the figure now ?"

" Oh, curse the figure, never mind totals, I have news worth half a million, provided I have your help."

" I know what you mean ; but there's no reliance to be placed upon the reports about the Mortimers."

" I know better. I will tell you to-night. I expected to meet only you here, for I saw your worthy dad half-an-hour ago going off to the city, so I came on to see you, for there's no time to lose. I will leave you now. Mind and be punctual to-night. By the bye, what's in that immense iron chest let into yonder wall ?"

" Ah, that's father's sanctum sanctorum. It contains wills and important deeds ; the house might burn down, but the contents of that chest would be quite safe."

Mr. Delme stood a moment, regarding it with a steady look and a half smile on his handsome features. He was a tall and exceedingly well-made man, dark, clustering hair, fine complexion, and hands remarkably small, and delicately white. Though extremely handsome, and with large, dark, restless eyes, there was a peculiar formation of the mouth when at rest, that gave a somewhat sinister expression to his features, but his countenance must have been caught at rest, for an observer to notice this peculiar expression, for in general his features were continually undergoing change.

"Well, adieu, John," said Mr. Delme. " By-the-by, Sir Edgar's life is nearly run out, he won't stand the wear and tear of another week. Should like to make your pretty sister Bella Lady Herbert Delme—eh? what would the old boy say?"

" Why, faith, to tell you the truth, he would say—No, she should never be Lady Delme with my consent.''

" Ah, never mind; once Lady Delme, and backed by nearly half-a-million, it will matter very little how he will receive his re-

pentant son-in-law—ta! ta!—don't be very
late to-night."

Shaking John Calthurst by the hand, Mr.
Delme passed out, closing the door after him.
He had a well-appointed curricle waiting for
him at the door; but, as he walked through the
office, one of the clerks, a young man of some
six or seven and twenty years, got up and
accompanied him to the door. In the hall
Mr. Delme said, in a low voice, " In that iron
chest, I suppose."

" Yes," returned the clerk, whose name
was Thomas Adams.

" Very good!" returned Mr. Delme, " be
punctual to-night—eleven o'clock, to the
minute, for I am to meet John Calthurst at
twelve."

" All right," said the clerk, and proceeded
on down the street.

Mr. Delme paused at the hall door, looked
at the two handsome iron greys in his splendid
curricle, laughed, and then humming a tune,
he sprang in, took the reins, and drove off.

CHAPTER V.

THE month of March set in, as it usually does in our changeable climate, cold, stormy, and every way uncomfortable. Mr. Calthurst had written to an old friend, a solicitor, practising in Plymouth, begging him to spare neither expense nor trouble in making enquiries from ships of war entering that port concerning the fate of the passengers taken from the Cumberland Packet aboard the Droits de l'Homme, and also to learn, if possible, the names of all the English saved from the wreck of that ship in Audierne bay, especially if a family of the name of Mortimer were saved—mentioning the members of the family to consist of father, mother, son, and daughter, and two female domestics. Up to the fifth of March, all the intelligence he had received was a confirmation of the previous rumour that the Cumberland Packet was taken by the French seventy-four, and her passengers transferred to the Droits ; but on the nineteenth of March he received the following letter from the Plymouth solicitor—

" My dear Friend,

    " It grieves me to find I must put a final close to your sanguine expectations that any of the unfortunate family of Mortimer were saved from the fearful wreck of the Droits de l'Homme."

Mr. Calthurst laid down the letter, and buried his face in his hands, and remained so for several moments. He was greatly grieved and affected. " Alas! not one," he murmured to himself several times. " I could not bring my mind to believe in such a fearful and tragical ending to my dear old friend, and his,

I may say, young wife and family. He had a prophetic feeling, I do think, pressing upon his mind when he wrote his last letter to me; but let me see how it came to pass." Taking up the letter, he continued—" Two days ago there arrived in this port a vessel from Brest, full of English prisoners released by the government of France, and sent to England without ransom or exchange. These persons were all landed, and I soon learned that the captain of the Cumberland was one of the number. I immediately waited upon him at the Crown Hotel. Captain Inglis gave me all the particulars of his unfortunate capture, and horrible sufferings when shipwrecked in the Droits de l'Homme; but as Mrs. Heartley, Mrs. Mortimer's attached attendant, was one of the saved, and, after terrible sufferings, was taken aboard a French gun brig, carried to Brest, then released and sent to Plymouth, will be able to give you minutely all the particulars, I refrain from the subject. I have furnished her with funds and every requisite, and she departs to-morrow for London. This is a sad business—Mrs. Mortimer and boy got safe to land; but the child was unable to rally from the privation of proper food for three days, and died. This loss, and her own sufferings, brought poor Mrs. Mortimer to death's door—a fever carried her off, and she was buried at Quimper. Mr. Mortimer saw his daughter safely embark on a raft, but, from want of strength, and being in a kind of stupor, he was unable to follow; Captain Inglis states that those on the raft undoubtedly perished in the surf, and Mr. Mortimer was found, when assistance arrived on the fourth or fifth day, insensible—he was taken on board a French vessel, and, on arriving at Brest, died, and was buried with every decency and attention, by order of the French commodore. I assure you this intelligence, my dear friend, though the parties were unknown to me, made me quite sad, and Captain Inglis himself says he can never forget the circumstances of that disastrous and melancholy voyage. He speaks in very high terms of the gallantry, courage, and devotion of a young gentleman, a midshipman, a passenger in the Cumberland, named Augustus Chamberlain, who, it is supposed, perished in endeavouring to save Mr. Mortimer's daughter, when the raft was overwhelmed in the surf. Poor Mrs. Heartley is fearfully cut up. She was eighteen years in the service of Mrs. Mortimer—left England with them, and now returns to her native land a wreck of her former self.

" Your sincere friend,

" H. J. HEAD."

Mr. Calthurst laid the letter on his desk, with a sigh, and remained plunged in painful thought for nearly half an hour. He was sitting in his private office in Welbeck-street at this time.

He then rose—unlocked a very handsome and massive cabinet, and from a secret drawer

took two singular keys, of intricate wards.
With these keys he unlocked the great iron
chest inserted in the wall—this chest contained an inner chest.   On opening this,
several   drawers   were   observable — each
drawer contained important documents and
papers.   Opening one that had the letter M
on the outside, in brass, he gazed at a parcel
of papers it contained.   He seemed to have
received a sudden shock as he gazed; then
he hastily turned them over.   As he did so,
the perspiration ran from his forehead.   Suddenly a slip of paper, with a few lines in
writing, caught his attention—his hand shook
with the terrible agitation that was overpowering him.   He could not at first read the
writing—passing his handkerchief across his
eyes, he held the paper to the light, and read,
in bewildered amazement and stupefaction,
the following words—"The last will and
testament of Henry Compton Mortimer, till
lately in this drawer, is now in safe hands,
and will be restored to Mr. Calthurst, safe

and uninjured, in consideration of a sum of ten thousand pounds. As this will devises a sum of nearly half a million, giving to Mr. Calthurst the sum of ten thousand pounds, in consideration of past services, and from sincere friendship, the amount demanded for its restoration is small. When the proper time arrives, Mr. Calthurst will hear from the present possessor of the will, and of the mode in which it will be returned, and how the ten thousand pounds must be paid."

Mr. Calthurst sank down into his chair, like a man whose brain had suddenly become affected—he seemed for a time to lose all consciousness of time, place, or circumstances. However terrible the blow, Mr. Calthurst was not a man, after the first shock was over, likely to give way and abandon any pursuit or object without a severe struggle. Recovering himself, he opened a cupboard, took out a decanter, poured out some wine into a glass and drank it. This seemed to revive him. Taking the paper, he looked minutely and carefully at the writing, and then shook his head. "A stranger's hand," he muttered, "of course." He then carefully examined all the drawers in the chest. Nothing appeared out of place. All the papers and deeds were as they were directed and numbered—the locks perfect, not the slightest trace of having been tampered with. "No," said Mr. Calthurst, "they were not picked or forced; they were opened by similar keys to these," and he keenly regarded his own keys. As he did so, something caught his eye between one of the wards. "Ha!" cried the lawyer, taking a pin, and picking out the small object. It was wax. "So," said he, "an impression was taken in wax; very good, that's one clue; but I never remember leaving those keys for five minutes at a time, and never being absent when I did so. Now, if anyone took the model of these keys he must have had access to my desk also, and the key of my desk is never off my watch chain. The next thing to be con-

sidered is, who benefits by the abstraction of
this will—Herbert Delme, of course; but
Herbert Delme once in possession of a document, which, by destroying, would just make
him master of half a million of property, is
not a likely person to take his grasp off of
such a sum for a paltry ten thousand pounds;
therefore Herbert Delme can have nothing
to do with its abstraction. Another thing
amazes me," he continued, soliloquising,
" I never mentioned having received
this will from Barbadoes to a single
human being, not even to my wife. Mr.
Mortimer forwarded it to me at the time
he remitted the produce of his Barbadoes
estates. He stated that he made this will,
having been prompted to do so by a strange
feeling he could not overcome. ' I may be
shipwrecked with all my family, and perish
on the voyage home,' said my poor friend, in
his letter. ' I would not, on any consideration,
that such a man as Herbert Delme should
inherit my fortune, to squander it in vice

and profligacy.' Excepting a few legacies, the
bulk of his wealth, therefore, in case of not
one of his own family surviving, was left in
charitable bequests, and in founding an hospital.

"Who, then, could possibly become acquainted with my having such a document
(witnessed by four gentlemen of position and
wealth at Barbadoes), in my possession—it's
mysterious."

Suddenly Mr. Calthurst recalled a circumstance that occurred on the very day he
received the packet containing the will of
Mr. Mortimer from Barbadoes. The packet
was brought to England in the Diamond
frigate, and delivered to Mr. Calthurst by
Lieutenant Holmes, of that ship. Lieutenant
Holmes was well aware that the carefully
sealed packet he delivered was the will of
Mr. Mortimer, for he was a personal friend of
that gentleman. Mr. Calthurst and the lieutenant had some conversation on the subject
of the will in his private office, and wanting
one of his clerks to go out on particular

business, instead of pulling his office bell, he went to call him himself, and on suddenly opening the door he found his clerk, Adams, with his hand on the handle. Mr. Adams looked quite unconcernedly into his face, saying, " I was just coming to ask you, sir, if you will attend the court to-day in John Williams's case; it is now twelve o'clock, and the court will close at two o'clock."

Mr. Calthurst had not the slightest suspicion of anything wrong. Mr. Adams was a favourite clerk, a protégé of his —he therefore said, " I was just coming to tell you to go to the court, and beg Mr. Henderson not to bring on the case till to-morrow. Hasten as much as you can, and deliver my request to him."

"I hope I shall be in time, sir," and the clerk hurried out of the office.

Now that Mr. Calthurst had brought this circumstance into his mind and thoughts, it was surprising how rapidly other circumstances, apparently trivial, followed on the first. He recollected that he had observed his clerk Adams several times come to the office exceedingly pale and haggard-looking. He thought at the time that he was ill, and suffered from confinement, and, naturally kind and thoughtful to those in his service, he told him he looked ill, and said he might take a holiday, and go into the country now and then. But a still stronger incident suddenly recurred to him—two or three months previously he was leaving his office hurriedly, being late for court, when the ring of his watch chain caught in the key of the door, in passing, and broke, scattering the keys and trinkets on the floor. Mr. Adams sprang from his desk, and picked them up; being in a hurry, the lawyer thrust them into his pocket, and hastened to court. When not engaged in the business of the court, he pulled out his seals, and, looking over them, he missed the peculiarly small but extremely intricately-warded key of his cabinet, in which he kept the keys of his iron safe. He felt no uneasiness, for he supposed it was lying on the floor, and he should find it on his return; but an hour afterwards Mr. Adams entered the court. and, giving him the key, said it had rolled under a side table.

As he returned home he entered a jeweller's, and purchased a strong ring, and never bestowed another thought on the circumstances. Now, putting one thing with another, and stringing them together, he came to the conclusion that Mr. Adams, his clerk, was open to suspicion. He and an old steady clerk, eighteen years in service, and one trustworthy female servant, who dusted and swept the offices, slept in the house every night. Mr. Adams was an orphan; Mr. Calthurst knew his father, and greatly esteemed him. He had seen better days, and wasted the latter years of his life and his little funds in a hopeless Chancery suit. Alas! how many even now follow this ignis fatuus—a Chancery suit—to the close of life, and die—hoping against hope to the last. Even now, as we write, the papers are full of a very distressing case—that of a poor woman dying from sheer starvation and cold, with three millions and a half due to her in the Court of Chancery. When old Mr. Adams died, he left his son at the age of eighteen to struggle with the world. He was a good penman and an excellent accountant. Mr. Calthurst took him into his office—he became, in two or three years, the favourite of father and son; and now, in his twenty-sixth year, was a confidential clerk, with a salary of two hundred and twenty pounds a-year. It pained Mr. Calthurst that any suspicion should attach to his favourite clerk, and he began to think that all these trivial circumstances he was torturing his brain to recollect might, after all, mean nothing. Still, the will was gone, and there was no illusion in the writing on the paper.

He could regain the will by paying ten thousand pounds. Now ten thousand pounds was a large sum; but half-a-million was a vast sum. "If I do not recover that will," he said to himself, "that wicked, profligate man, Herbert Delme, will get the whole of my lamented friend's vast fortune, to be spent in a life-long career of vice and profligacy."

Suddenly an extraordinary idea entered Mr. Calthurst's brain. He started up, saying, " I'll do it," and rang his bell.

If in the office, Mr. Adams always answered his bell—accordingly, in a minute or two he entered Mr. Calthurst's private room. Richard Adams was a very prepossessing-looking young man, about the middle height, dark blue eyes, very light brown hair, and a slight graceful figure. He dressed well. At this time he looked somewhat pale, and his eyes had a dark shade under them.

Mr. Calthurst, with a cheerful expression of countenance, looked up into Richard Adams's face, saying briskly—" Well, Mr. Adams, I have made up my mind *you* shall have the ten thousand pounds; but I must have the will before six hours are over, and you must leave the country in twenty-four."

Before Mr. Calthurst had finished the sentence, Richard Adams staggered back—his face becoming livid, then, clenching his hand, he struck his forehead wildly, and, uttering a fearful imprecation, rushed madly from the room.

Mr. Calthurst remained rooted to the floor —his eyes fixed upon the door, as he exclaimed, " Ah! I've found the robber; but a thousand to one, I've lost the will." Then he hastened through the passage into the office. The other clerks were standing in a group, looking stupified ; but Richard Adams was gone. Mr. Calthurst said not a word, but putting on his hat, he also left the office, and hurried to Bow-street. An hour afterwards half-a-dozen active officers were in pursuit of the culprit Richard Adams.

When Mr. Calthurst joined his family at their usual dinner hour all were present, except his son. Mrs. Calthurst and her daughters could perceive that something unusual had happened to him—he looked flushed, was nervous and agitated.

" My dear," said his spouse, " has anything unpleasant occurred to-day? you look heated and over-excited."

" Where is John?" asked Mr. Calthurst.

" He was here an hour ago," replied Mrs. Calthurst, " and said he was going to dine with young Gardener—they had made a party for Covent Garden to-night. By-the-bye, Mrs. Heartley, poor Mrs. Mortimer's attached attendant, has arrived from Plymouth, by the mail. She could not come here to-day, for she is still very poorly; to-morrow she hopes to wait on you. What a dreadful misfortune, my dear. I suppose, and very naturally, the terrible and deplorable fatality that has destroyed the whole of the Mortimer family, has exceedingly affected you."

" I wish John had not gone out this evening," said Mr. Calthurst, abstractedly, " Where is Mrs Heartley staying?"

" At the Saracen's Head," said Mrs. Calthurst.

" Let a room be prepared for her to-morrow," said Mr. Calthurst, " and now come
to dinner, a glass of wine will do me good.
Afterwards I will talk to you about this sad
affair."

The dinner passed over with very little
conversation on any subject; but the dessert
on the table, and Mr. Calthurst, somewhat less
excited and agitated, commenced the conversation by apologising to his wife for not
answering her questions when he first came
in.

" The fact is as you surmised; this
terrible catastrophe of the Mortimers has
knocked me to pieces. I never grieved so
much in my life. I may as well tell you, for
now it will be no longer a secret.

" Mr. Mortimer sent to me from Barbadoes
a packet. It was delivered to me by an officer
of the Diamond frigate, to whom I wished
to shew every attention, and invited him to

my house, for he was a fine, handsome, dashing sailor; but, unfortunately, he had to leave London at once for Portsmouth, to join another ship. He was second lieutenant of the Diamond, and he was made first lieutenant of the Arethusa. In the packet sent me was the will of Mr. Mortimer."

" Will!" exclaimed Mrs. Calthurst.

Had Mr. Calthurst looked into his youngest daughter's face, he would have perceived that she turned exceedingly pale, and looked startled.

" Dear me!" continued Mrs. Calthurst, anxiously, " What caused Mr. Mortimer to send a will to you, and he coming home himself, and with his family?"

" For that very reason, my dear," said Mr. Calthurst, " he made his will, thinking that it was possible that the ship might founder or be lost, and perhaps all might be drowned. He wished to guard against such a contingency—he seemed to have had a presentiment hanging over him—it's nothing unusual; many men have had the same feeling."

Mrs. Calthurst appeared confounded, whilst Bella actually trembled with agitation; the eldest daughter was unconcerned.

"Then he could will away his entire property from the next heir," said Mrs. Calthurst, as her husband helped himself to wine.

"Most certainly he could, and did."

Bella's pretty lips were positively colourless; but she held her handkerchief to her face.

"He was firmly resolved," continued Mr. Calthurst, "that the wealth accumulated by his father and himself should not fall to the lot of one who would have squandered it in vicious propensities, and wilful profligacy."

"Well," said Mrs. Calthurst, somewhat bitterly, "the old adage has some truth in it —'Give anyone a bad name, and no after act will clear it away.' The world, or at least you and several others, give Mr. Herbert Delme a very bad name."

"You think so, my dear, because you know nothing about him," returned Mr. Calthurst, rather surprised. "You appear inclined to defend him. You have seen him only in respectable company; but I have, unfortunately, been mixed up in transactions in defending two or three clients, that will not bear the light, and in which Mr. Herbert Delme figured conspicuously. However, as we have nothing to say to Mr. Herbert Delme—"

"He became Sir Herbert Delme, this morning," interrupted Mrs. Calthurst, emphatically, and, perhaps, rather triumphantly, for Mr. Calthurst, looking around him, said—

"Well, all I hope is that neither of my daughters will become Lady Delme."

"Indeed, papa," returned the eldest daughter, "it's a speculation, I am sure, that never entered my head."

"In truth this is a very hard and harsh

world," said Mrs. Calthurst, " and it is very strange how forcibly we preach of Christian principle and feelings, and how very rarely we forgive one another ; but nourish antipathies and hatreds to the last moments of our lives against our fellow creatures who have once sinned, and are willing to repent and amend their lives; the world remembers only what they were, and scoffs at their repentance."

" I hope not, Mary. I hope not. I do not think this is at all a universal feeling," said her husband. "I am sure if Sir Herbert Delme turns over a new leaf, and leads an honourable and virtuous life, his early faults will be freely forgotten and forgiven; but we must be satisfied that such a change has happened. However, we have strangely wandered from our subject of conversation What I have now to tell you is this—the will sent me by my deceased and lamented friend has been stolen, abstracted from my iron chest."

" Good Heavens!" exclaimed his wife, in unmistakable astonishment, " stolen ;" whilst

Bella's eyes flashed, and her cheeks glowed with excitement behind her handkerchief.

" Then," continued Mrs. Calthurst, " if the will has been stolen, and cannot be recovered, Mr. Mortimer's intentions in making this will will be frustrated. Who could have committed this desperate act, and how could that iron chest of yours, that you have often declared could neither be picked, burned, nor broken open, have been opened, and the will taken out?"

" Ah!" said Mr. Calthurst, " we can all boast, and our strongest measures be over-turned by a straw. My chest was neither picked, burnt, nor broken into. It was opened by the keys made for it, and the man I most trusted and favoured is the one who betrayed me. Richard Adams is the culprit, and the police are now upon his track. I trust in God he may be taken, and the will recovered."

Miss Bella Calthurst who had, during this conversation, undergone a singular change of feelings and sensations, now filled a glass with water, saying, " I have been suffering a most disagreeable tooth-ache all the day. I must go and put some laudanum to my gums.   I think I have a severe cold."

" I hope not, my child," said the father, affectionately, " your face does look flushed; put a piece of flannel round it."

The two daughters retired, leaving the old couple earnestly conversing.

CHAPTER VI.

Our readers, will remember that we left our young heroine, Annie Mortimer, and Augustus Chamberlain, on the beach of the bay of Audierne, some eight miles from the wreck of the Droits de l'Homme. The wind and tide had driven the raft in a slanting direction along the shore, and towards a spot where the surf, owing to sandbanks, broke with terrific violence. In the spray and mist raised by the gale, the sea appeared to those on the deck of the seventy-four in the distance, to swallow up the raft and its unfortunate crew. But such was not the case—it was turned over certainly; but the undaunted hearts who trusted their lives to its frail support, struggled with the furious surf, and gained the shore.

It was a narrow, shingly beach bounded by lofty craggy heights. On a projecting cliff— above where those on the raft made the shore—was a fort and battery, mounting four twelve pounders. The captain of the fort, with his fourteen artillerymen, had watched the raft making for the beach. Now it unfortunately happened that Captain Renaud Popatin was a most violent revolutionist, and a furious enemy of the English. He was quite aware, having sent two of his men to the scene of disaster the day before, that the wrecked ship was a French seventy-four, and the other wreck an English frigate. He, of course, thought those on the raft must be French; and, therefore, with half-a-dozen of his men, and a score of peasants from the heights, ran down to the beach to assist his countrymen. Not that Captain Renaud Popatin had one spark of humanity in his little shrivelled carcase.

He was a small, thin man, with a harsh, cadaverous face, smothered in whiskers and moustache. Every second word he uttered was an oath; and his vanity was so great, that he fancied he bore a strong resemblance to Bonaparte, under whom he had served in two campaigns in Italy, beginning his military career as a drummer; so, at all events, he must have shewn not only courage, but some little skill, to have gained the rank of lieutenant, though he permitted himself to be called captain, since his appointment to the command of the important, as he called it, battery of Pierre Point.

Dashed ashore by the boiling and roaring surf, Augustus Chamberlain staggered up the beach, with the light form of the girl in his arms, whilst the five English seamen made the land some fifty yards lower down, and nearer to Captain Popatin.

In a moment the Frenchman perceived that the sailors were English. " Ah! sacre bleu," he exclaimed to his men, " they are English; make them prisoners at once. March them up to the fort. I will go and see who those two are that have got ashore higher up."

Half-a-dozen of the country people and four of the artillerymen seized the exhausted and half-drowned sailors, and instantly carried them off to the fort.

Our hero seated himself on a rock, supporting the half-drowned and nearly exhausted form of Annie Mortimer in his arms. Her long and abundant hair was loose, and hung about her person in large tresses. She was fearfully pale, and trembled all over from cold and terror, but she was quite sensible.

"Oh, Augustus!" she exclaimed, "what horrors we have gone through—you have perilled your life to save mine. You are exhausted, and, alas, here I shall die. I feel that I shall die, and never see my adored mother, and father, and brother again."

"No, no, Annie," returned her preserver, "you will not die. God has mercifully preserved us thus far; He will still shield us.

See, there are persons coming along the beach. We will carry you to some house or cottage."

As Captain Popatin came up with his four artillerymen on one side, a gentleman, in the costume of a chasseur, having a fowling-piece in his hand, and followed by four dogs, came rapidly up on the other. This new arrival was a tall and handsome man, perhaps six-and-thirty, or thereabouts. Captain Popatin, however, reached the young couple first. Our hero had just time to whisper " I will say we are brother and sister, dear Annie—it may save us from being separated."

" Oh, do so, Augustus," replied the trembling and nearly insensible girl, " to be separated from you now would be my death."

The Frenchman looked at the young couple evidently with great surprise. " You are English," he at length said.

" Oui, monsieur," returned our hero, " we are."

" Then you are my prisoners," and, turning

to his men—he had not yet perceived the stranger—he said, "Take these English to the fort, and separate the female from the rest of the prisoners."

"We are brother and sister," interrupted our hero, angrily, "Do not you see the sad state this young lady is in?"

"Sacre tonnerre! do you dictate to me?" returned Captain Popatin.

"Stay, monsieur," interrupted an authoritative voice, "there is no occasion for this severity; I will take charge of this gentleman and his sister."

Captain Popatin turned round astonished; but the moment he beheld the stranger, he doffed his hat, saying respectfully, indeed humbly, "Mais, monsieur le general, they are those pestilent Anglais."

"Well," returned the stranger, with a smile, his eyes fixed upon the intensely pale but beautiful features of the girl, who gazed into his face, with a feeling of hope stealing into her heart—"though they are

English, they will not eat us. Now, my lads,
come here," calling a dozen gaping peasants
to his side. " Now, my lads, make a kind of
hammock of your blouses, and carry this unfortunate maiden to the chateau,—it is time
she should receive assistance. But first,
mademoiselle," continued the stranger, taking
a flask from his pocket, " take a little of this
cordial which will support you, till you reach
the chateau ;" filling out half a wine glass of
brandy, he persuaded Annie to swallow it,
and it did send a slight colour for a moment
to her check.

Our hero thanked the stranger warmly and
gratefully.

" The same in a larger dose," returned the
gentleman, " will do you no harm," and he
handed him the flask.

It was a grateful draught to our hero, and
he stated as much. Captain Popatin stood,
looking somewhat mystified, till, Annie being
lifted by our hero into a temporary litter, the
men began to move off with their burden.

" Now, Monsieur Popatin," said the stranger, " come here," and he stepped aside, whilst our hero walked by the side of Miss Mortimer. " You have several English prisoners, Monsieur Popatin, have you not?"

" Oui, monsieur," returned the commander of the Pierre Point battery, " I have six."

" Tres bien.   Just send three of them to Quimper, keep the other three strictly confined at the fort, and as to this brother and sister, say nothing about them.   You understand me, eh ?—you know what I promised you."

Captain Popatin bowed low.   " You shall be obeyed, monsieur le general."

" Bon jour, captain."   He pronounced the last word with an emphasis, and then walked rapidly after our hero and heroine.

Having overtaken the litter, he said, addressing our hero, after taking a very scrutinizing survey of his person and features, which seemed to surprise him.   " I have not heard the full particulars of this sad wreck.

How came so many English to be on board, monsieur ?"

Augustus Chamberlain briefly related how they had been captured, and how the Droits had fought the two English frigates, and, being disabled, was driven ashore in the gale.

"One of the English frigates was wrecked, I hear, and at no great distance from the Droits," returned the stranger.

"Yes, monsieur, the Amazon, the smaller of the vessels."

"You are, I suppose, an officer in the navy," continued the stranger, "to judge by your garments?"

"Yes, monsieur; but I can only rate myself a midshipman, though appointed a lieutenant; for, as yet, the appointment has not been confirmed." He then, in a few words, stated how he had been wounded at Santa Cruz, and, drifting in a boat out to sea, was taken in a Spanish vessel to Barbadoes. The Frenchman seemed interested, and as our hero concluded, they came in sight of the Chateau de Haute-

ville, the residence of the stranger, whose
name was De Hauteville.

The chateau was a huge pile of building,
like all the chateaux of that period, and like
a great many at this moment in the remote
province of Britanny. Immense piles of
chimneys, high peaked roof, covered with
bright red tiles, with long avenues of trees,
leading to the principal entrance. A terrace, a
fountain, and several statues, formed the ornamental portion of the front entrance.   Numerous domestics were summoned when the
cavalcade, with the now insensible Miss Mortimer, entered the hall.   The housekeeper, a
fine stately old dame, with a very benevolent
countenance, made her appearance, and to her
care Annie was consigned by Monsieur de
Hauteville, with orders to use the warm bath
and restoratives, and then to wrap her up
and immediately to put her in bed.

Augustus Chamberlain let Annie's cold
hand drop from his with a sigh of regret,
and a look of profound sorrow.

"Nay, monsieur," said De Hauteville, who was observing him with a somewhat singular expression of countenance, "you need not be alarmed for your sister's life. She will rapidly recover when properly treated, and she shall have the best of care."

"I deeply feel your kindness, monsieur," replied our hero. "She has suffered terribly for four days, and her mind, I am satisfied, suffers more than her body—the uncertainty she remains in respecting her parents tortures her."

Our hero did not perceive the smile on Monsieur de Hauteville's lips, as he said "her parents;" but he had no longer the intention to keep up the deception of being Miss Mortimer's brother. It would, he felt, be useless.

"It is time, monsieur," said the owner of the chateau, "that you change your soaked garments; though you are so young. there is little difference in our stature," and, summoning an attendant, he desired him to conduct the

Englishman to a chamber, and to take him every necessary article of clothing he required. " When you have changed your clothes, and taken a glass or two of wine, we will dine— a meal, I dare say, that will be acceptable to you."

Our hero bowed, and returned the hospitable Monsieur de Hauteville thanks, and, greatly surprised, in truth, somewhat mystified, followed the domestic up a grand staircase, across a gallery, and into a large lofty chamber, furnished in all the massive pomp of the times of Louis the fifteenth.

" I will bring you a change of linen, monsieur," said the domestic, "and a shooting dress of my master's—they will fit you well, to-morrow your own will be dried, and fit to put on."

" Thank you," replied Augustus Chamberlain. " What is your master's name and title ? "

" His name, monsieur, is De Hauteville—he was a marquis, and was also a general."

" Is he married?" our hero ventured to enquire.

" No, monsieur, he is a widower," and then he retired, but presently returned with an abundance of clothing.

" Well," thought our hero, " all this is very strange. This generous hospitality, and to enemies of the republic. It is very clear, my entertainer possesses power in this part of the country."

In the meantime, Monsieur de Hauteville entered a very handsome saloon, furnished in the prevailing taste of the day. On the tables, and scattered over the room, were various articles, betokening the use of the saloon by a female, a piano and harp, guitar, music on the side tables, and various articles of women's taste in those days—some seventy years ago.

Monsieur de Hauteville paced the chamber, seemingly in deep thought; he then suddenly sat down, and drawing a desk to him, took out writing materials, and commenced rapidly writing. Whilst so engaged, the door opened, and a young lady entered the room. She was not more than two-and-twenty, tall, graceful, and elegant in her attire and manner, with features, if not strictly perfect, yet exceedingly fascinating in their expression, with dark expressive eyes, and a profusion of rich auburn hair.

" Who on earth, uncle," said the lady, taking a chair, " is this beautiful girl—child, I might almost say—that you have brought here half dead and insensible. She would not have lived another hour without help, and that of the tenderest kind."

" Has she revived?" asked Louis de Hauteville, looking up anxiously into his niece's countenance.

" She has revived, certainly; and Dame Godelet is exerting all her naturally kind qualities to solace her; but she raves about father, mother, and brother, and some one she calls Augustus, and who seems to be very dear to her—her brother, I suppose, for she is too young to have a lover."

" Ha," murmured Monsieur de Hauteville, " I am glad she revives. Not that I feared a fatal result; though I knew the shock she has received might rende: recovery long and difficult."

" Restoration to health will be long and difficult," replied his niece. " But who is she? I know she is English, and that she was saved from the wreck of that unfortunate man-of-war; but why she is brought here, and only some of the other prisoners with her, surprises me."

" Why, Eugenie," said Louis de Hauteville, " you would not let her perish, or be handed over to the tender mercies of Captain Popatin, and conveyed to prison like the other miserable wretches saved from the wreck?"

" Mon Dieu! no," returned the French girl, with a flush over her handsome features. " I would not trust a pet dog to your protégé, Monsieur Popatin. No. I will do all in my power to restore this charming-looking girl to health. Is she to be given up to imprisonment afterwards; and where is your other guest—where is he?"

"You are somewhat curious, my dear niece," returned Monsieur Hauteville, with a smile. "Well, after all, it is but natural. As to my male guest, all I know of him is what he tells me, that he is in the navy—a midshipman, holding the rank of lieutenant, and that he is the girl's brother. At least, so I heard him tell Popatin, whom you call my protégé. He must be a youth of gallant spirit, and undoubted vigour, for he swam through a tremendous surf; and I think, my fair niece, if your heart were disengaged you would run a good chance of losing it, for this youth is singularly handsome, and with a noble figure."

"What?" returned the French demoiselle, laughing, "give my heart to a heretic, and a bitter enemy to your model republic?"

"Hush!" said the general, "the young Englisman is coming down the stairs attired in a suit of mine. Parbleu! for a youth of twenty, he is fitted well in my hunting suit."

Eugenie de Morni turned; the door of the saloon was open, and the grand staircase faced it. Augustus Chamberlain was then crossing the hall, a domestic shewing him the way to the saloon. Mademoiselle de Morni looked at the tall, elegant figure of the midshipman with surprise, and a great deal of interest. She had expected to see a well-grown lad, by her uncle's description, and now she beheld a young man fully as tall, and nearly as muscular, as her uncle himself. He became the handsome green hunting suit he wore; but was exceedingly pale, his features clouded, and wore a sad and thoughtful aspect.

As the youth entered the saloon, he beheld Eugenie de Morni, with a look of surprise, and bowed low. Monsieur de Hauteville rose saying—"This is my niece, Mademoiselle de Morni. I leave you to make each other's acquaintance, whilst I change my dress—we will then to dinner." He then left the room.

Our hero took a chair, and, seating himself, said, as he looked earnestly into the face of the French girl, " May I enquire, mademoiselle, for my companion in misfortune, Miss Mortimer, who has been so kindly and hospitably received into this chateau. I am deeply anxious about her."

" I can imagine so, monsieur," returned Eugenie, " is she your sister?"

" No, mademoiselle, she is not—neither is she a relative; but she is dearer to me than life."

There was a something in the tone, the manner, and the look of Augustus Chamberlain that forcibly interested Eugenie de Morni.

" I am happy to tell you, monsieur," she returned, " Miss Mortimer has rallied, and, I have no doubt, will eventually recover. She suffers as much in mind as in body. I understood from my uncle that you were her brother."

" When we were cast half-dead upon the beach, mademoiselle," said our hero, " with the certainty of being made prisoners, the harshness of a Captain Popatin, who announced that we were prisoners, and to be separated, induced me to say I was Annie's brother, hoping to be allowed to watch over her during her terrible trials; but I trust her mother and little brother are, though prisoners, alive, and recovering from the sufferings they experienced. Miss Mortimer's father we were, unfortunately, forced to leave behind, for the raft broke adrift before he could, in his weak state, be put on it."

" You have, in truth, monsieur," said Eugenie, exceedingly interested, " gone through great trials, the harder to be borne when your voyage was so nearly accomplished in safety; but, as far as mademoiselle's welfare and health is concerned, you may depend that every attention shall be lavished upon her. She is almost a child in years, keenly sensitive, and deeply attached to her parents."

" Thank you, mademoiselle," said our
hero, warmly, " I shall never forget the kindness we have received. The more you know
of Miss Mortimer the more you will be
charmed with her, for she is gifted, for one so
young, with an energy and strength of mind
and intellect truly surprising. She bore her
own sufferings without a murmur, cheering
her poor mother, whose only thought was the
safety of her children."

Eugenie de Morni looked serious and
thoughtful; but before she could reply Monsieur de Hauteville returned, and almost
immediately they proceeded to the dining
room, where a well-served dinner awaited
them.

Though our hero had scarcely touched any
food, save a biscuit and a very small quantity
of water, for several days, he felt too exhausted and weary in mind and body to do
justice to the good things before him.

" You speak French so well, Monsieur
Chamberlain," said Mademoiselle de Morni,

" that I could almost fancy you came from a distant province, and were a Frenchman."

" I was, when young, mademoiselle, taught by a French gentleman, who took great pains with me; and afterwards I had good practice in speaking as an interpreter at a French settlement."

" Your ships, Monsieur Chamberlain," said Eugenie's uncle, " were very severely handled in that unfortunate attack, by some of your most skilful commanders, upon Santa Cruz?"

" Pardon me, monsieur," returned our hero, " our ships were not engaged at all. We attempted the assault of an almost impregnable place with our boats. As to me, I do not know to this moment how the assault ended. I was engaged in the attack upon the sea ramparts from the quay; but we were mowed down like sheep by the terrible fire from the ramparts that commanded the whole length of the quay. I was nearly the last left alive on the wall, when a musket shot threw me off the quay."

" I can tell you how the affair ended," said Monsieur de Hauteville, " for it made a sensation in Paris, and, I confess, considerable rejoicing. Four or five commanders such as Nelson and Trowbridge failing in their attack was something new. The English were forced to surrender to the Spaniards—those who got ashore, and into the town; but, singular enough, your gallant countrymen actually demanded terms of surrender, such as conquerors would demand after a victory, and the Spanish governor acceded to them. Thus, droll enough, they returned to their ships, and left the place unmolested; but your renowned Nelson lost an arm, and several superior officers were killed and wounded. Pray, what ship did you belong to, monsieur?"

" The Leander, fifty-gun ship," returned our hero. " I trust Captain Thompson's name was not amongst the killed or badly wounded?"

" Thompson!" repeated De Hauteville,

thoughtfully. "No, there was no name like that—let me see. Ah, now I remember, there was a Captain Bone, or something like that."

"Ah! you mean Bowen, Captain Bowen, of the Terpsichore frigate—alas! is that gallant spirit quenched?"

"Yes, that is the name," returned Monsieur de Hauteville. "I remember the name of the ship."

"But how," exclaimed Eugenie de Morni, "did you escape, monsieur, after being wounded, and remaining, even till now, ignorant of the fate of your ship or your comrades?"

Our hero briefly explained to the French demoiselle what is already known to our readers. She seemed greatly interested; but plainly perceived that our hero was overcome with weakness and weariness. She at once said, "I think, monsieur, you must be greatly in need of rest, and the very best thing you can do is to seek repose."

"You are right, Eugenie," observed Monsieur

De Hautville, summoning a domestic, " I was very wrong in not thinking of this sooner; but a good night's rest will greatly restore you."

" You are very kind, monsieur," said our hero, rising. " I am worn out, and, but for your generous hospitality, my sufferings would have been tenfold greater." Then, wishing mademoiselle good night, and shaking hands with monsieur, he followed the domestic to the chamber prepared for him.

After the departure of our hero, uncle and niece remained seated near a blazing log fire for some time without speaking. At length Eugenie looking up into the very serious countenance of her uncle, said—

" I suppose, Louis, I must postpone my departure till this poor girl recovers sufficiently to be restored to her parents."

" I shall feel obliged by your doing so, Eugenie. Your mother will not be at Coulange for a fortnight at least, so there is no hurry." He hesitated a moment, and then continued, "This girl's mother will never recover—she is dying."

"Mon Dieu! how do you know that, uncle," asked the French girl, looking serious.

"I have had full particulars from Quimper this morning, with a list of the passengers and English prisoners saved from the Droits. It appears that Mrs. Mortimer and her infant son were saved in a boat manned by English sailors; the child had suffered much on board the wreck, and died eight hours after landing. The mother, already reduced by suffering, became distracted, and the authorities imprudently moved her, with the rest of the prisoners, to Quimper. She was seized with a dangerous fever, and I hear has no chance of living till to-morrow."

"God help the unfortunate child we have here, then—this intelligence must be kept from her, or it will kill her."

"Such is my wish," returned De Hauteville. "But Louis," interrupted Mademoiselle de Morni, "what are your projects with respect

to this girl and her lover.   He is most de-
votedly attached to her, I can easily see."

"Bah!" interrupted Monsieur De Hautville, "what is a child's attachment—she
will forget this love in a twelvemonth;
and as to the young man—who ever heard of
a midshipman being in love for three months
at a stretch.   He is easily disposed of.   I will
send him to Quimper to-morrow, or the day
after."

"No, Louis," said mademoiselle earnestly.
"You cannot act so cruelly.   Why profess so
much kindness—treat him as a guest, and
then hand him over to captivity."

"Just order in the coffee, my dear niece,
and whilst we are sipping it I will let you
into a secret that will explain all to you."

Shortly after, the coffee was placed on the
table, poured out, and the servants retired.
Monsieur drew his chair closer to his niece,
and, after a moment's thought, said—

"I remember, Eugenie, telling you many
strange things of my unfortunate grandmother,

the late Marchioness de Coulange. You
then laughed at me, and said the old woman
was mad, and that her prophecies were wild
dreams. I was angry, and said no more at
the time. But I now tell you that what you
call ravings and wild dreams were, without a
doubt, the inevitable decrees of fate, and the
prophecy she uttered is now working
itself out."

An incredulous smile sat on the lips of the
French demoiselle; but she remained silent.

"You very well know, Eugenie," continued Monsieur de Hauteville, "that I am
the last male descendant of one of the noblest
houses in France—with me perishes the name
of De Hauteville. But I tell you, and my
information comes from an undoubted source,
that the time is rapidly approaching when
our titles and our grandeur will be restored.
It is notorious that my ill-starred grandmother,
when on the scaffold—which she mounted
in her seventy-eighth year, with the heroic
fortitude of a martyr—with her last breath

I 2

prophesied, that a man would rise out of the ashes of our wasted republic, who would put his foot upon the necks of the people of France, and instal himself on the throne with a power and grandeur greater than ever a Bourbon possessed; but that even he should be swept from his throne, and perish miserably. I saved your mother and yourself from the same fate as my unfortunate grandmother; but her I could not save."

"I know all this," said Eugenie, sadly, "and how, dear uncle, you risked life to save your sister and me from the monster, Marat. But, alas! your grandmother's senses fled after the execution of the poor queen; and her prophecies were the mere ravings of an unsound mind."

"No, niece, they were the promptings of fate. Is not a part of that prophecy already accomplished. I tell you, I firmly believe, before another year expires, that Bonaparte, our present consul, will be a crowned king. However, let time work its way. Now listen

to her predictions before she went, as you state,
mad; but first I will tell you a remarkable
incident—you will call it a legend—of our
ancient house."

CHAPTER VII.

"WHEN Henri Quatre," began Monsieur de Hauteville, finishing his cup of coffee, " was king of France, Philippe de Hauteville, our ancestor, was lord chamberlain, and greatly beloved by the king. Some days or weeks before a vile assassin robbed France of a good king, Philippe de Hauteville, at a very late hour, left the king's chamber, and was retiring along a gallery that led to his chamber in the palace, and had just reached the door, when he suddenly perceived, standing right before him, a tall figure, muffled from head to foot in an immense roquelaure.

" Surprised at seeing anyone in that part of the palace at that hour of the night, he laid his hand upon his sword, and, as he held up his lamp, he said, ' Who are you, sir, that intrudes here at such an hour?'

" ' I am one,' exclaimed the stranger, ' interested in the noble house of De Hauteville. Before many days elapse, a royal head will be laid low by the dagger of an assassin. If you wish to save your life, and your name from unmerited disgrace, quit France in four-and-twenty hours, and retire to your estates.'

" The marquis, in a rage at hearing this strange prophecy, instantly attempted to seize the unknown; but the lamp in an unaccountable way was dashed from his hand, and the corridor became involved in darkness. Not liking to create a disturbance in the palace at that hour of the night, he entered his room, found his valet asleep before the fire, and the lamp expiring. Rousing his confidential attendant, he lighted a wax taper, and went out into the corridor. He picked up the

dropped lamp; but no human being was to
be seen in the corridor.

"Where, my dear Louis," said Eugenie,
" have you picked up such a wild legend?"

" It is no legend.   It is to be read in valuable manuscripts I saved at the sacking of
Chateau Coulange," said De Hauteville, " but
mark the result."

" My ancestor, it seems, paid little heed to
this warning, but it appears he spoke of it in
a somewhat bantering tone to some of the
courtiers.   But the day foretold came, Henri
Quatre fell by the dagger of the regicide
Ravaillac.

"When Philippe de Hauteville heard this
horrible news, he became bewildered, and
the following day was arrested and at once
hurried off and incarcerated in the Bastile.
The marquis's son was at this time with the
army in Flanders.   When he heard of his
father's imprisonment, on a supposed charge
of being concerned in the assassination of the
King, he left the army and returned to France.

On reaching Paris he boldly demanded justice for his father, and that he should be brought to trial and heard. The King at once assented, but the next day the unfortunate marquis was found dead in his bed. It was stated by the physician of the Bastile, that he died from over-excitement, and a rush of blood to the head.

"For a whole generation the De Hautevilles were exiles from the court of France, remaining on their estates in Brittany and in the Vaude. But during the reign of Louis the Fifteenth, they again appeared at Court, and after a time regained their former position, and in after years another Philippe de Hauteville became a great favourite with the royal family. Now it appears very strange that each marriage of the heir of De Hauteville produced only one son, but several daughters. My grandfather had but one son, and, as you know, I am an only son. 'Louis,' said my grandmother to me one day. I was then about twenty-two or twenty-three years of age. 'Louis,—You will have no children, except under one condition, and think of that, and the house of De Hauteville, six hundred years old. The De Hautevilles will become extinct.'

" ' I hope not, grandmother,' said I, ' for I am going to marry Anne de Chilli. '

" ' Yes,' said she, ' but you will have no children.'

" At that time I thought little of her predictions; but in four years I was a widower and childless. Three years afterwards I wedded the young and beautiful Justina le Croix. There was a fearful fatality in my marriages. Young, healthy, and of pure blood, Justina, whom I fondly loved, lived but six years. I was again a widower, disconsolate and childless. When my noble grandmother was seized and condemned, and ordered for execution, for her determined affection and loyalty to our ill-starred Queen. I was permitted to see and take leave of her. She was perfectly resigned and undaunted,

' Why grieve for me, Louis, ' said she, ' what could I expect after living seventy-eight years but death, and perhaps, a lingering and painful death.   The guillotine has no terrors for me —a brief second, and my soul will be before my Maker—but listen to my last words.   I have seen the stranger who predicted Henri Quatre's assassination to your ancestor, who was barbarously murdered in the Bastile, by order of the King's prime minister.   A fearful time is coming, but, as I told you before, France will rise triumphant from her degradation—but let me speak of yourself.   You have been twice wedded, and are childless. The house of De Hauteville can only be saved from extinction by your marrying a foreign maiden, a castaway, and of a country always hostile to France.   This is the decree of fate, and inevitable. '

"Guards entered the prison; I embraced my venerable grandmother with overpowering emotion, and, as the soldiers separated us, she called out,

" ' Remember, Louis, and promise you will, when the opportunity occurs, fulfil the destiny of your house.'

" ' I promise,' I exclaimed, and the next instant she was torn away."

Louis de Hauteville paused, and cast a scrutinizing glance at his niece, who had listened to the recital of her uncle without a word of interruption. There was a long pause, and then Louis de Hauteville said,—

" Do you now comprehend the motive that has actuated my present conduct?"

" I can very readily imagine, uncle," returned Eugenie, in a very serious tone, and looking troubled, "that you have let the words of your poor grandmother make a deep impression upon you."

" Deep impression!" repeated Monsieur de Hauteville, with exceeding earnestness, "believe me, the traditions of my race have eaten into my heart, and the words of my grandmother are written in characters of fire upon my brain. When first I beheld this girl,

who lies between life and death in the very
chamber so often occupied by my grandmother, for in that chamber she was born
—I say, when I first looked into the pale,
worn, but lovely face of that child, as her
head lay upon the breast of the youth who
called himself her brother, I was struck with
a strange and overpowering feeling. Me-
thought the last words of Madame de
Coulange were hissed into my ear—'Remember your promise.'

"My thoughts were as rapid as the electric
fluid. I said to myself, this girl is a castaway, and she comes of a race ever hostile to
France. Here is my destiny. This is the
motive which induced me to act as I have
acted. Now do you understand my plan."

"Alas! Louis, I perfectly understand this
wild and impossible project. You dreamed of
making this child your wife, for a child in
comparison to you she is, and with her heart
devoted to another. Have you considered for
one single moment the innumerable obstacles

that stand in the way of so wild, and I may say, so insane a scheme? Even if this poor girl's mother dies, her father may live, and her lover lives, and I know in my heart, Louis, your nature is far from cruel; you have brooded over wild rhapsodies till—"

"Nay, Eugenie," interrupted Monsieur de Hauteville, hastily and angrily, "I will listen to you, and even yield somewhat to your judgment, which I have seen, under trying circumstances, is sound and discriminating; but I will not permit the solemn words of the dead, spoken in the hour of doom, to be treated irreverently. My project is neither wild nor unattainable. Miss Mortimer is too young for serious attachments. I intend to place her for two years under the care and protection of your mother, who has, like myself, implicit faith in the prophecies of my grandmother. At the expiration of two years she becomes my wife."

"And what is to become of that brave young man, Monsieur Chamberlain, who idolizes this child in years, but with a woman's heart. Will you destroy his happiness for ever, and crush his memory from this girl's heart. You cannot do this, Louis; no, no, you have too noble a nature to become a—"

"Silence, girl, I will no more of this romantic nonsense," fiercely exclaimed Monsieur de Hauteville. " You try me too far. I tell you this once for all, I will carry out this resolve, or perish," and, without another word, Louis de Hauteville left the saloon.

Eugenie de Morni's cheek flushed as her uncle left the room; he had spoken harshly to her for the first time. She would have felt deeply grieved at this at any other moment. She loved her uncle sincerely; to save her and her mother from the doom of many an aristocratic head in those troublesome times, he had perilled life and fortune; she knew he possessed in reality a most kind and liberal disposition, but she also knew he was a man of strong and fiery passions, and that, once resolved upon a project, no obstacles would turn him from his pursuit. A personal and attached friend of General Bonaparte, with whom he had served in Italy, and gained, when scarcely more than twenty-two years of age, the rank of general of brigade, he quarrelled with a superior officer, and in a duel nearly killed his antagonist. A severe rebuke from Bonaparte, then in command of the army, caused him, in a fit of passion, to throw up his commission and retire from the army.

The thought, too, of the house of Hauteville becoming extinct, preyed upon his mind, for, with all his superior intellect and understanding, he was a firm believer in destiny, and placed implicit faith in the delirious ravings of the old Marchioness de Coulange, who was notorious for her prophecies and denunciations. Eugenie therefore felt satisfied, now that he had so strangely met with a female, who in his mind forcibly came up to the prophecy of his grandmother, being English, a castaway, and an enemy to France, he would yield to no persuasion, allow no obstacle to interfere with his determination.

" If," said Eugenie to herself, " I can save him from the commission of what is certainly a great crime, without shame or reproach being cast upon his name, I will do so—these young people interest me much, and I cannot help thinking this poor child will be both mother-less and fatherless; if so, her whole love of existence will be centered upon that young lover of hers."

After remaining some time in thought, she rose, and, taking the light, proceeded up the grand staircase to visit the invalid before retiring to rest.

Upon a bed in a lofty and strangely fur-nished chamber—for Monsieur de Hauteville would not permit the heavy antique, but splendid furniture of the room to be removed— lay Annie Mortimer; a bright log fire in the immense hearth gave a cheerful look to the otherwise gloomy chamber. Eugenie gently drew back the curtains, and gazed with deep interest upon the pale calm features of the girl.

" She is sleeping," she said to the house-keeper.

" She has a sweet pretty face," the dame replied.

" Yes," answered the French demoiselle, emphatically.   " She   is   very   lovely ; such   a   face   once   seen   is   not   easily forgotten ;   and   if   Louis,   who   saw, and considered   her,   when   half   drowned, and pale as a corpse, beautiful, what will he think when he sees her in health ? Alas ! I fear there is trouble, and sorrow, and trials for that fair being to undergo.   She is young to feel the passion of love ;   but Monsieur Chamberlain is just the age when romance lends to the passion an intensity overpower-ing ; he loves this girl as a child.   How will it be a few years hence ?"

Dropping the curtain, she approached the

fire, and sat down. "How long, Dame Morelle, has she been asleep?" asked Eugenie of the housekeeper.

"More than three hours, mademoiselle. I really thought at one time she would not come round. She's a pretty young creature, and over young for such trials, mademoiselle."

"You are right, dame, and I fear, besides the trials she has endured, she will have greater to suffer. They say her mother will not survive, and her little brother is already dead."

"Oh! Bon Dieu! have mercy upon the poor thing. If you tell it to her now, it will kill her." A shriek rang through the room, so heart-rending, so piercing, that Mademoiselle de Morni's heart beat painfully, and she trembled greatly, as the curtains were dashed partially aside, and Annie Mortimer threw herself wildly from the bed, and, dashing herself on her knees before the horror-struck Eugenie, exclaiming—

"Oh, take me in mercy to my mother—my

own beloved mother.   She is dying, I heard
you say. Oh, God!" and she threw her arms
wildly into the air. " I saw her. She is
dead!" and the young girl fell, as if struck
down, totally insensible on the floor.

Her piercing shriek had rung through the
chateau, and struck terror to the inmates.
Monsieur de Hauteville heard it as he was
ascending the stairs. Alarmed, he rushed on,
and entered the chamber as the housekeeper
and Eugenie were lifting the insensible and
unfortunate girl into the bed.

"Mon Dieu! how is this? what is the
matter?" exclaimed De Hauteville, gazing
bewildered upon the corpse-like features of
Annie Mortimer. "She is dead.   Grand
Dieu! is it so ?"

"No, no," said Eugenie, impatiently.
"Leave us. She has only fainted. We
thought her asleep, and we spoke of her
brother's death and her mother's illness. Pray
leave us, Monsieur de Hauteville."

Monsieur de Hauteville stood as if powerfully excited by some peculiar feeling, and then exclaiming, " It is destiny—it cannot be helped," cast one more look at the inanimate face before him ; and left the room.

CHAPTER VIII.

AUGUSTUS CHAMBERLAIN fortunately did not hear the shriek that disturbed so many in the Chateau de Hauteville that night. He rested in a remote chamber, and slept a sleep that would have required the report of a cannon to disturb. When he awoke in the morning, a domestic brought him his own garments, and stated that his master awaited.him in the saloon, where breakfast was on the table. Anxious to hear how Annie Mortimer had passed the night, he dressed himself in a few minutes, and was crossing the gallery to the great staircase, when he encountered Eugenie de Morni. As he saluted her and politely returned her kind enquiries, he said, " I trust, mademoiselle, that Miss Mortimer is somewhat restored to-day after a night's rest, and also that tidings have been received of her mother's safety and health ? "

As he asked the question he observed that Mademoiselle de Morni looked rather pale, and that the expression of her countenance was sad.

" Mademoiselle Mortimer," said the French maiden, " is still very weak and ill; anxiety concerning her family retards her recovery. It will take some time to restore her."

" If reunited to her family, Mademoiselle," observed our hero, " her health would rapidly improve. She has a fine constitution, and great fortitude."

As he spoke the words, they entered the breakfast saloon. Monsieur de Hauteville was pacing the room backwards and forwards. Seeing the midshipman, he held out his hand, saying, as he looked into his face, " I am glad to see that a night's rest has made a great improvement in your looks. One would scarcely imagine you had borne four days' starvation, and other suffering besides."

"In our profession, Monsieur de Hauteville, we are accustomed to many vicissitudes, and hard trials of all kinds; our constitutions get hardened; so if we are down one day we are up the next. Have you heard, monsieur, from Audierne or Quimper?"

"Sit down and do justice to the fare before you, Monsieur Chamberlain," said De Hauteville, "and we will converse afterwards. In most situations in life, rough or smooth, and I have experienced enough of both to be able to speak confidently, a man bears himself always better after breaking a fast of twelve hours."

Augustus Chamberlain sat down beside Eugenie de Morni. There was an ample and well-furnished table; coffee, fruit, pasties, game, and choice wines. During the meal Monsieur de Hauteville turned the conversation upon subjects foreign to existing circumstances. He spoke of the state of France, of the war with England and the chances of peace. He insensibly led our hero to converse of his early life, and the various scenes he had been engaged in. Eugenie was unusually silent; but she listened with great interest to what Augustus Chamberlain said. Just as breakfast was over, a domestic entered, saying that Captain Popatin wished particularly to see Monsieur de Hauteville.

"Request the captain to walk in here," said De Hauteville.

"Then I think, Monsieur Chamberlain, you and I had better retire," said Eugenia de Morni, looking by no means pleased.

"Well, as you please," remarked her uncle; "go out through those glass doors and take a turn in the gardens; this redoubtable captain will not detain me long."

The large window of the breakfast-room reached to the floor, and led into a handsome, well-arranged garden; it was not exactly the time of year to see a garden in its beauty, let it be ever so well laid out. Eugenie de Morni led the way, and Augustus followed, and both disappeared as Captain Popatin, bowing and grimacing, entered the saloon.

"Sit down, Popatin, sit down," said De Hauteville, "and help yourself to a few glasses of Lucerne or Chambertin, it's a raw morning, and the gale scarcely subsided yet."

Captain Popatin accordingly sat down and very willingly drew a flask of Lucerne towards him, and filled a glass with the sparkling wine.

"Well, Popatin, what has occurred during the night?"

"Monsieur, not much; the two vessels anchored off the wreck have sailed with all the people they could save. Those saved are all here, except three, who, according to your desire, are still in the fort; the rest were marched to Quimper."

"In your report you have, as I requested, left out the young naval officer and his sister."

"Oui, monsieur, they are not mentioned."

" Bien," returned De Hauteville, " you may reckon on having your captain's commission before a month is out."

Popatin was in ecstasies; to be called captain, was not exactly being a captain, and receiving a captain's pay.

" Do you think a boat can put to sea to-morrow from our creek, provided the weather moderates ?"

" Most undoubtedly, monsieur," returned the captain. " The wind has shifted, the two vessels anchored off the wreck led out of the bay safely ; the sea is falling rapidly."

" Well, then, all you will have to do will be to take care that none of your men sight the boat running past the fort to-morrow night. I am anxious it should not attract anyone's attention."

" Rest satisfied, monsieur. None in the fort shall see the length of their noses; of course you will excuse their being too drunk to see. Half my men are gone with Sergeant Dempriere to Quimper, and the remainder, excepting four, retained in the fort, I will send on an expedition to Audierne to watch that nothing is plundered that comes from the wrecks."

Whilst this conversation was taking place, Eugenie de Morni and the midshipman were walking in a sheltered part of the garden.

" I beg of you, mademoiselle," said Augustus Chamberlain, " to let me know what you have heard respecting those unfortunates saved from the wreck. I can see plainly by your countenance that something has happened to disturb you, and, if I am not a very bad judge of human nature, I should say yours is a feeling heart, and that you are above disguise of any kind."

"You are flattering, monsieur," said Eugenie, with a faint smile ; " however, you are, alas, correct in your surmises. We have had tidings from Audierne and Quimper, and I deeply regret to tell you Mrs. Mortimer's infant son has died from the effects of all he suffered in that ill-fated ship."

"My God!" exclaimed the midship-
man, tears, despite every effort to conceal
them, stealing down his bronzed cheek.
"Little Charlie dead,—the child I loved so
dearly, and would have sacrificed a dozen
lives to save, —and his young innocent life is
sacrificed. Alas! mademoiselle, my sorrow
is great, pardon this weakness. After all,
man is in some cases as weak as a woman.
I have seen death in all shapes. Death in all
its horrible forms, but that sweet child's
death unmans me."

Eugenie de Morni had as susceptible a
heart as ever beat in the breast of a woman.
She gazed at the young sailor, as he passed
his handkerchief across his face. She read
every thought of his heart, and she said to herself
—"She who first wins the love of this youth
will holds it whilst life last. He will never
love another, but will love, cherish, and save
her. He does love, and will love, with all the
fervour of his ardent nature."

"Pray, mademoiselle," said Chamberlain,

after a pause, " have you heard how the poor mother bears this fresh and to her terrible misfortune. Little Charley was the mother's and father's only hope and joy ; for him was the father's vast wealth intended; for him they delayed their departure from Barbadoes —fatal delay! Had they sailed in the Racehorse frigate, as intended, all would have been saved."

" Man proposes, but God disposes," said Eugenie, sadly. " The mother, alas! is in a dangerous fever, and Mademoiselle Mortimer having heard intelligence not intended for her to hear just now, has half the night been passing from one hysterical fit to another. I never left her side till they in a great measure subsided."

Augustus Chamberlain felt as if struck to the earth. Suddenly taking the French girl's hand, he said, his voice choked with emotion—" Mademoiselle, I have scarcely the power to utter in words the feelings of my heart. I confess to you that the happiness of

my whole future life is wrapped up in that
apparent child. When her mother quitted
the wrecked ship, with despair in her heart,
and a foreboding of evil agonising her soul,
prostrating her more than even her sufferings
had done, she said to me—

"I go to save my boy, and thus abandon
husband and daughter. To you I leave my
child; if you are saved, she is yours. Cherish
her as you would your life."

"Then," said I, as I lowered her into the
boat, "we live or die together.

"She is as yet little more than a child in
years; but to her my destiny is linked irre-
vocably. I shall be removed to Quimper to-
day or to-morrow, and months, perhaps years,
may elapse before I regain my freedom. Miss
Mortimer will thus, if her father and mother
cease to exist, be utterly alone. May I im-
plore you, as far as lies in your power, to afford
her your protection till she can be restored
to her own country. If her father survives,
but, alas! I left him in a fearfully exhausted

state, of course he will seek and recover his child, till then, shield her as far as lies in your power, and may God in his mercy and goodness protect her, and reward you for your acquiescence in my wishes."

Eugenie de Morni listened to the midshipman's appeal to her heart in favour of the English girl, with considerable emotion. She had felt a singular interest in the young man from the very first interview. In his manly, simple, kind-hearted nature, there was no disguise, every emotion agitating his heart could be read in his open interesting countenance.

" You may rest satisfied, Monsieur Chamberlain," said Mademoiselle de Morni, " that the young lady shall receive every attention, and that I will devote my energy to insure her restoration to her country; and till that can be done she shall not quit my sight, except a force is applied that I cannot resist. I do not think she will be claimed by the authorities as an English subject, and be detained a captive ; for my uncle has great authority over this district, and Captain Popatin, the only person aware of her being in the chateau, would not on any account act contrary to his wishes. Mrs. Mortimer may recover, if so, it will be easy to let her know where her daughter is. She will, of course, demand her restoration, and the authorities will grant her request. But here is Monsieur de Hauteville. Under every circumstance, you may depend on me."

Kissing the hand he pressed, in acknowledgment, he thanked the kind hearted French demoiselle from his heart.

When Monsieur de Hauteville joined them, Eugenie left them, returning into the house.

" I am rather puzzled how to act," said the count, as they sauntered down the long avenue of the garden, well gravelled, and bordered on each side by trellised vines, which in the proper season, covered the long walk with a delightful shade. " You must go on to Quimper with Popatin to-morrow, at furthest. I have insisted on that delay. They are sending all the prisoners to Brest. Mademoiselle Mortimer is totally unable to go; to move her would kill her, I shall be able to save her from this journey, till restored to health, and some clearer account of her parents is received. Till an account comes from Brest, we cannot know who was saved from the wreck of the Droits, by the two ships anchored there yesterday. I had a lettter this morning from Quimper, and I am surprised to hear that they are acting with much rigour to the English prisoners, and that they may expect a long captivity, the government being greatly incensed, indeed infuriated, by the total failure of the grand expedition to Ireland. Most of our fine fleet has been dispersed one way or another, and this loss of a favourite ship the Droits, adds to the feeling of exasperation against your countrymen."

"I am careless as to my own fate, Monsieur," said Augustus, after a moment's reflection, " as a prisoner I cannot assist the

unfortunate daughter of Mr. and Mrs.
Mortimer, and that is the sole object of my
thoughts. What will become of this young girl,
I ask you, Monsieur de Hauteville, as a
gentleman and a man of honour," and he
looked steadily into the Frenchman's face.

"Well, Monsieur Chamberlain," returned
De Hauteville, " thus far you cannot find fault
with what I have done to serve you both."

" God forbid I should be ungrateful, Monsieur de Hauteville," interrupted our hero,
hastily, and with a flush on his cheek, "you
have been most kind and generous, and for
the kindness we have received, accept my
warmest and heartfelt thanks; but when I am
taken away to-morrow, and consigned to a
prison, Miss Mortimer, who is, I hear, exceedingly unwell, will remain, entirely de-
pendent on your help and assistance, to restore
her to her father or mother if they live. Should
neither, which God forbid, be in existence, what
then will become of this bereaved girl; to be
sent to a prison would kill her."

" She will be perfectly safe under the care
and protection of my niece, Eugenie de
Morni, who will shortly be proceeding to join
her mother, my sister, a woman of as kind
and noble a heart as any in existence, and
quite independent. Her husband, the Count de
Morni, fell defending his King; his wife and
daughter would have perished under the
guillotine, but the party I espoused were at
the time all-powerful, and after a fierce
struggle, during which they underwent many
singular adventures, I got them safe into
the country. After the fall of Robespierre,
things changed, and now Madame de Morni
has had part of her husband's estates restored,
and lives retired in Chateau Morni. I propose,
when Mademoiselle Mortimer is able to
travel (should she not be claimed by her
parents), that she shall accompany my niece,
and remain under the care of Madame de Morni
till you get to England, and make some enquiry after her friends, for relatives or friends
she must have, as her father, you say, possesses

great wealth, and there must be some agent in England who attends to his affairs."

"But should I remain in captivity for any lengthened period," said our hero, "my power of serving this poor girl will be small indeed. Your kindness and generosity, Monsieur de Hauteville, I duly appreciate, and warmly thank you."

"I have all this day," said Monsieur de Hauteville, "been thinking of a scheme that would, if it succeeds, be a great benefit to you, and enable you to materially serve Miss Mortimer. Let us suppose you had an opportunity of escaping, and a means offered you of getting to England, would you feel inclined to make the attempt?"

The young man started, and the flush of excitement coloured his cheek as he said, "Most undoubtedly I would, monsieur. As long as I remain a prisoner, I can be of no earthly service to anyone, but let me once reach England, I feel satisfied I should be able to set her father's confidential agent to work to effect both her release and that of her parents if still alive."

"Well, I certainly think the benefit would be worth the risk; if it fails, you will only be a prisoner, as before," said De Hauteville, thoughtfully, " Monsieur Mortimer may live; it is quite possible. If so he will be carried to Brest, but I candidly tell you I have very little, if any, hope of Madame Mortimer surviving. One English lady has died, I understand, since her removal to Quimper. Their sufferings must have been terrible on board that ill-fated ship."

"Terrible, indeed," observed our hero, sadly. "Strong men gave way the second day, and the third they sunk;—but in what manner, monsieur, could I possibly escape, and reach the coast of England?"

"I will tell you how it is possible to manage it," said de Hauteville, "but you must not hint at it in any way before my niece. I am one of those who cannot believe that a woman can keep a secret, and this project of mine must not be breathed to a human being."

"You wrong the sex, Monsieur de Hauteville," returned the midshipman, earnestly.

"Ah! mon ami, you are young; before you reach my age it is possible you may think otherwise. My niece is a noble hearted, generous girl. She is engaged to a gallant officer, and must not be made a party in this somewhat dangerous affair."

" Not for any consideration, monsieur," said our hero, "would I involve either you or mademoiselle in any peril."

" There will be no peril or difficulty in carrying out my plan, as long as the particulars are confined to ourselves. I will now explain to you how my project of escape may be carried out.

" About two miles from the chateau, there is a sheltered creek, and a rough stone pier. In this little creek, which dries at low water, I keep a small, fast-sailing lugger, of about twenty tons. I use her for occasional sea trips in the summer, but have not yet hauled her up, or taken her sails out ; would you, if you had two or three of your own countrymen, all sailors, attempt the run across the channel in so small a boat, at this season of the year."

"I should not feel the slightest hesitation in making the attempt," said our hero, greatly surprised, "but in getting out of this bay, a boat must pass close under the battery, where we were cast ashore. We should be perceived."

" Do not trouble yourself about the battery of Pierre Point. Monsieur Popatin is devoted to me; I can make or mar his fortune; he shall be blind. Confined in the fort are three English sailors, three out of the six who came ashore with you on the raft; they were to be sent on to Quimper this morning, but I prevented their departure. You have interested me, and I wish to give you a chance of escape, instead of losing the precious years of your youth in a dreary captivity."

"You are generous, Monsieur de Hauteville,"

said our hero, really affected by the kindness
of an enemy.

"You would doubtless do the same for me,
were I placed in a similar position," replied
the Frenchman. "Everything shall be in
readiness for your escape to-morrow night. I
will provide provisions for a few days, and will
let it be known that I am going to have a
look at the wreck of the Droits. The three
sailors shall be in readiness, the boat will
float about ten o'clock, and you can clear
the bay long before daylight. You must keep
well to the northward, mind that, and there
is no doubt you will fall in with one of your
own cruisers, for the port of Brest is now
beset by British ships-of-war. We have no
cruisers nearer than the Penmarks; one or
two small ones keep off those rocks, but as
your course is to the northward, you will run
no chance of being chased by them. To-
morrow I will take you a walk after breakfast, show you the creek and the lugger, so that
when you leave the chateau at midnight, you

will easily know your road to the creek. So now, till I have completed my arrangements, let us say no more about it. We will go in, and, remember, not a word before my niece."

As they entered the chateau, our hero told Monsieur de Hauteville, that he was most intensely anxious to see Miss Mortimer; he should then be able to judge what hope there was of a speedy recovery.

"There can be no objection, that I can see," said De Hauteville, "I will send for Dame Morelle, who will let us know whether the excitement would be too much for the young lady. By-the-by, should you see her able to converse, there will be no harm in stating that you have a hope of getting to England, where you can be of more service in arranging for her and her parents release, than remaining for months in a prison, where you will be forced to go if you remain here ; only caution her not to speak of this to any one."

Just then Dame Morelle entered the room.

" Well, dame," said Monsieur de Hauteville,
" how is your young patient."

" She is very low indeed, monsieur," returned the housekeeper, " she persists in
thinking her mother is dead, and is constantly
praying to see monsieur, her brother."

" Then take monsieur to her at once, dame.
I sent for you for that purpose ; the sight of
one dear to her may have a beneficial
effect."

" It will do her more good than a doctor,"
said the housekeeper, " for the mind, more
than the body, is killing her. Mademoiselle
Eugenie is with her now."

" Then please go with Dame Morelle," said
De Hauteville to our hero, and he abruptly
left the room.

Our hero, exceedingly agitated, followed
the housekeeper, and shortly arrived at the
door of the sick chamber.

" Just stay a moment, monsieur, I will tell
her that you are coming, so that she may not
be too suddenly excited."

Augustus Chamberlain had not long to waste in anxiety; the door re-opened, and Mademoiselle de Morni came out, saying, "You can go in, monsieur, but pray avoid exciting subjects, give her hope; having hope she may live; destroy it and she dies." She then descended the stairs, and our hero entered the room, and closed the door.

We have said that the chamber was a very lofty one, with antique furniture, grand and massive; the bed was of the time of Louis XV., several feet from the floor, of great width, and surmounted by a carved canopy and plumes of feathers. Lying in the middle of this immense bed, was the once fair form of Annie Mortimer.

Dame Morelle had drawn back the heavy curtains, and partly raised the blinds of the windows, so that some portion of light fell upon the pale, worn features of the sad girl. Her large and still beautiful eyes, but sunk into the head, were turned, with an expression of intense anxiety, towards the door, and her thin transparent hand extended from the bed, as if anxious to grasp that of one she dearly loved.

When Augustus Chamberlain's eyes rested upon the invalid's face, and he beheld the terrible change her sufferings of mind and body had wrought in so short a time, he felt as if his heart had ceased to beat, so fearfully unnerved was he. A change came over her countenance as she beheld him, his face pale from overpowering anxiety and grief, whilst, bending over the bed, and holding her little hand in his, he pressed his lips to her pale, cold forehead, saying,

"Ah, my poor Annie, what you have suffered;" he could not restrain his tears, which fell fast upon the wasted cheek of the young girl.

"Do not weep for me, dear Augustus," said the maiden, in a low voice, "for I shall soon be happy with my own loved mother and our little Charley. Thank God, I have seen you once more."

" But Annie," and Augustus exerted himself to check the trembling of his voice, " you
are giving way to despair, you have frightened
yourself into the belief that your dear,
mother is worse than she really is."

" Ah, Augustus, and do you, too, try to de-
ceive me. I know my mamma no longer lives."

"On my soul, you are in error, Annie,"
earnestly exclaimed the midshipman, " she is
ill, with fever from the terrible suffering she
went through, and the loss of her dear boy ;
but she is alive, and whilst there is life there is,
thank God, hope. Annie, love, rouse yourself
hope always, for God's mercy is infinite ; live
to bless your father and me, for, beloved
Annie, your life is mine, my only thought is
of you."

The sufferer closed her eyes, but tears
forced themselves beneath the lids ; whilst the
little hand that rested in his trembled with
emotion, and for a time neither spoke.

Gazing at the youthful pair, Dame Morelle
said to herself, " Ah, bon Dieu ! these young

folks are dearer to each other than brother and sister. She will recover yet."

Annie Mortimer, after a time recovered from her exhaustion and emotion, and then said, "but tell me, Augustus, how it is that we are left to the care of these kind people. I have seen, in reality or perhaps in my dreams, a young and very beautiful face bending over me, and looking like a pitying angel; is it really a dream?"

"No, dear girl, you have seen Mademoiselle Eugenie de Morni, the niece of the generous gentleman who has afforded us his protection."

"Then it was no dream. I am so glad, I thought I heard a voice say my mother and brother were dead, and then I shrieked wildly, and threw myself from my bed, and knelt at some one's feet; but I fainted, I suppose, for afterwards it seemed to me a dream, foretelling my beloved mother's death. Now I have hope, I will struggle to overcome this terrible

feeling of desolation, and of being all alone
in the world."

"My poor child," said the midshipman,
"and did you think I would desert you whilst
life remained to me?"

"No, no, Augustus, I never thought that;
to you I twice owe my life, and, whilst life
lasts, you are to me all the world after my
parents. But when you are taken away as a
prisoner will you think of me, and never
forget me, even if years fly by, and we do
not meet."

"Forget you, Annie, never, so help me
God! never, whilst life lasts; but listen to
me now, for you must not exhaust yourself by
speaking.

"To-morrow I am to be taken to Quimper,
and detained a prisoner; for how long, God
only knows; it may be till this war ends. Now
the generous owner of this chateau is a
gentleman who has great power; he was before
the revolution one of the nobility; he offers

me the means of getting to England at once."

"Oh dear Augustus," anxiously exclaimed Annie, " go directly ; here you can render us no service. Once in England, papa's agent, Mr. Calthurst, will immediately take steps to release us, by paying money as ransom, or some such means. Do you not think so."

" Yes, dearest, I do," said the midshipman, " and for that very reason I have resolved to get to England as quickly as possible. Could I remain here and watch over you, I would oh! how gladly, stay. But to-morrow I must either leave as a prisoner of war, or adopt the means of escape provided for me."

" Do not hesitate a moment, Augustus ; once in a prison, God knows when and how you would get out. I feel myself safe with that beautiful sweet face that looked so kindly upon me, and which I thought came to me in a dream."

" Annie, darling, I must not let you talk any more, you must regain your lost hope and courage, and rest satisfied that every thought and action of my life will be for you and your happiness."

" Ah, dear Augustus, you have given me hope. I feel even now better; I am after all but a child, and know but little of the world. My adored parents were my world, and when you saved my life I joined you to them, and thought of nothing else, and wished for no other world than our own circle."

" Farewell, my own Annie ; " said her lover and, stooping, he kissed her fondly, and pressing the little hand to his heart, he rose to retire. Annie felt inclined to weep, as she saw him leaving, but looked cheerful as she could.

Turning to Dame Morelle, our hero said, " I have great hope, dame, that a few days will restore your patient to some of her former strength."

" I think and hope so, monsieur," said the housekeeper, " she has frightened herself; but now she has seen you, and heard all you could tell her, her mind will be relieved, and that relieves the body when no serious malady exists."

Taking a last look at the now calm, resigned face of the invalid, who waved her little hand to him, our hero left the chamber.

CHAPTER IX.

" We will take a walk to the sea-shore, Monsieur Chamberlain," said De Hauteville, after an early breakfast the following day, when Eugenie had retired and left them together.

Leaving the chateau, they proceeded down the long avenue in silence; but when they began ascending the hill that hid the chateau from the sea, Monsieur de Hauteville said—
" I have everything arranged for your departure, and you see the weather is now moderate, and the air not so cold, so that you may count upon a southerly breeze, which will run you out of this bay without any risk."

" There does not appear to be any risk to a craft of twenty tons or more," said our hero, " in navigating the bay of Audierne. The bank on which the Droits struck, and which I see by an old chart in the breakfast saloon, stretches to within half a mile of the west shore, has abundance of water at all times of tide for a vessel drawing eighteen, or even twenty feet water. This depth of water it was that made the situation of the Droits so terrible; the rollers came in with such stupendous force."

" I can imagine that," said De Hauteville, " for the water outside that bank is of great depth."

Passing through a defile in the hills, they soon came upon the sea-shore. Down this little valley ran a strong stream of water, which, entering the bay, formed a small creek, which a long range of high rocks protected from the high surf that generally ran in upon that iron-bound coast.

Lying moored in this creek was an ex-

tremely handsome lugger of twenty tons burden. She was just then left dry by the
receding tide. It was near sunset, and
though the wind blew moderately from the
south-west, to the experienced eye of the
midshipman, the weather did not look by any
means pleasant. A ground-swell also ran in
on the beach, and fell upon the rocks pro-
tecting the creek with a dull, moaning sound.

"You see," said Monsieur de Hauteville,
"that there is a cable run out from the lugger
to a buoy outside the rocks; by this she can
be hauled out, so as to clear all, after setting
sail. I am partial to the sea, and during the
summer months I use the lugger. But for
my present intention, and the use I design for
my little craft, she would be unrigged, and
hauled up out of reach of the tide. Higher
up the bay you may see some houses on the
cliff, and below them several fishing-boats
hauled up—that is the hamlet of Pierre
Point. On your right hand is the battery.
You see, by keeping this shore in running

out, you will avoid all the banks that line the coast to the southward. Steering south-and-by-west out of this bay in the night is very dangerous; but the course to the northward is clear, and you will have daylight to steer clear of the islands and rocks that lie direct in your course up the Channel."

" Yes," returned our hero, " you are quite correct. I have been cruising off Brest, and am aware of the intricate navigation amongst the islands and numerous reefs and rocks ; but by steering north they may all be avoided."

"I am am glad you know the coast, but you must be careful, and keep a steady course north; should the breeze be fresh, and you make too much way, you could, after running out some three or four leagues, lie-to till day-light."

After some further conversation, on the same subject, our hero and his host returned to the chateau.

During dinner Mademoiselle de Morni was unusually silent; she, however, stated to our hero that Mademoiselle Mortimer was considerably better, and looked forward with hope. "Alas!" continued Eugenie, "I dread the arrival of our messengers from Brest and Quimper."

"Whatever intelligence they bring," said Monsieur de Hauteville, "unless indeed satisfactory, must be kept from Miss Mortimer's knowledge."

Our hero looked very sad, for he felt exceedingly anxious, and dreaded evil tidings. "What time, Monsieur de Hauteville," he asked, "do you expect your messengers?"

"They may arrive at any moment," he replied. "I have a letter or two to write, so, pray excuse me for a time. My niece will, no doubt, compensate to you for my absence." He then left the saloon.

"You have been to the sea-shore, monsieur," said Eugenie. "Our coast here is neither very romantic nor picturesque."

"The coast of Brittany, I believe, is not accounted very picturesque?"

"No," returned the French demoiselle, "it is not. Nevertheless, there are some spots sufficiently beautiful to repay a visit. Where I intend going the coast for several miles is exceedingly romantic, and Chateau Coulange is admirably situated. It is there I propose carrying Mademoiselle Mortimer till her ransom or parents or guardians take steps for her exchange."

"I cannot sufficiently thank Providence in thus affording Miss Mortimer such protectors," said our hero. "It may never be in my power to thank you again, mademoiselle. My profession as a sailor during war time renders life exceedingly precarious. I may never live to see this poor girl, who is so dear to me, restored to her parents or her country. But for the kindness we have received accept my warmest gratitude."

Eugenie de Morni looked very serious; she remained for some moments silent, with her eyes bent on the carpet, but suddenly looking up with a more cheerful expression of countenance, she said—" We must, or rather we should do well, to look upon the bright side of the picture. I have had myself many hard and severe trials to go through. In fact, after being condemned to death, for no other crime than being strongly attached to the unfortunate Princess Lamballe, and in the bitterness of my heart expressing my sentiments to her cruel oppressors, I was brutally dragged before an equally brutal tribunal, and, after my condemnation, thrust into a filthy dungeon, to await my doom; and yet, Monsieur Chamberlain, I never gave way to despair—my spirit never sunk. To my uncle I owe my life. His unceasing efforts, aided by gold, and influence with the strong party, saved me and my mother from the axe of the guillotine. Monsieur Chamberlain, you too may hope to overcome the severe troubles that now darken your path." She arose as she spoke, and as our hero pressed forward to open the saloon door, she added, in a low tone and with marked emphasis—" This night be guided by the advice of an old sailor, and keep this advice to yourself." The next instant she retired.

Augustus Chamberlain remained standing by the door, surprised and puzzled—What can Mademoiselle de Morni mean? he asked himself. " Be guided by the advice of an old sailor"—What did those words signify ? Surely they were not a warning against the project of her uncle. Who was the old sailor? He could understand nothing; but he resolved to remember the warning, and wait for the solution. He then impatiently watched the arrival of the messengers, being intensely anxious to hear how Mrs. Mortimer was, and also to learn if Mr. Mortimer was amongst those rescued from the wreck of the Droits, and taken to Brest.

Just before dark a horseman rode into the courtyard of the chateau, and about twenty minutes afterwards, Monsieur de Hauteville entered the saloon with an open letter in his hand, and looking sorrowfully said, " I deeply regret to tell you, Monsieur Chamberlain, that Madame Mortimer did not rally, she died yesterday, in the evening."

"Good Heaven! what a sad event," exclaimed our hero, deeply affected. " My poor, poor Annie, what a blow this will be to your affectionate heart, no matter when it comes— soon or late ; the blow will be a crushing one."

" It is a sad tale of disaster, this wreck of the Droits de l'Homme," observed Monsieur de Hauteville, " there is many a heart made desolate by it. But you may depend on my niece to break this melancholy event tenderly to your young friend. She must be much stronger before she learns her bereavement."

Augustus Chamberlain was oppressed beyond all control; he could scarcely restrain his tears, or ask Monsieur de Hauteville if he had heard from Brest.

" I see," said his host, " that you take this sad intelligence much to heart, my dear sir. I trust, however, that Miss Mortimer's father may be one of those taken in the brig and cutter to Brest. My messenger has not returned, but I heard from Audierne that more than two hundred were taken safely out of the Droits. They can now communicate with the wreck from the shore; there is not a soul on board, and she is breaking up fast."

" I fear, then," said our hero, " that I shall not hear any intelligence concerning Mr. Mortimer."

" I fear not," returned De Hauteville, "my messenger is no doubt waiting the landing of those saved. I would," he added, in a low tone of voice, " willingly delay your escape, but after to-night it would be too late. I expect the mayor of this arrondissement will be here to-morrow. You I could not well detain. Miss Mortimer, from her age and sex, would not be disturbed, but left entirely under my protection till her release is ordered."

Our hero did not like to say much more on the subject. He saw that Monsieur de Hauteville appeared uneasy and restless; he therefore kept his thoughts to himself, and when Eugenie de Morni joined them at supper, he easily perceived that she had also heard the intelligence, and felt grieved at having to impart this sad event to her young protégé.

Very little was said during supper, Monsieur de Hauteville himself being exceedingly silent, and seemingly immersed in thought.

When Eugenie de Morni retired for the night, she wished our hero good-night with so peculiar a manner, and in so gentle and almost affectionate a tone, that De Hauteville started and regarded first his niece and then our hero, with a very peculiar expression of countenance. As soon as the former had retired, he said, fixing his eyes upon our hero, " I trust, Monsieur Chamberlain, that you have not given Mademoiselle de Morni any hint of your departure to night."

" I never forfeit my word, Monsieur de Hauteville," said our hero, very seriously. "No word has escaped my lips on the subject."

" Pardon me," returned the Frenchman,

more cheerfully. "I thought some inadvertent word might without your intending it have escaped you. I have ordered my attendant to place a pilot coat and a few necessaries in your chamber; now we had better separate, but as soon as our people are retired for the night, I will come for you, and conduct you myself as far as the descent to the beach."

" I trust we may some day meet again, Monsieur de Hauteville, when I can thank you for all the kindness I have received at your hands; this war cannot last for ever."

" I trust so, Monsieur Chamberlain," returned De Hauteville, " I shall be glad to renew our acquaintance."

When the young man reached his chamber, he placed his lamp upon the toilet table, and paced the chamber in a very troubled and thoughtful mood.

" I do not understand all this," he said to himself, " there is some deep mystery attached to this extraordinary hospitality and generosity of Monsieur de Hauteville. Why

should such excess of generosity be lavished
on total strangers, and upon natives of a
hostile country ?

He sacrifices his pleasure vessel, to ensure
the escape of an enemy, and for no other
visible reason than kindness of disposition. If
such is the case, then Monsieur de Hauteville
is a noble and generous gentleman. As to
his niece, she is above a motive, there is no
mistaking her pure and generous nature.
She has pronounced words that look like a
warning ; but how to take warning by them,
mystifies me. However, hope the best, and
trust in Providence. As he turned, a
gentle tap upon a door that was at the further
end of his chamber attracted his attention;
he had noticed that his chamber had two
doors, but had paid no attention to it.

As he approached, he perceived it slowly
opening, and before he reached it, it fell
back, and he beheld Dame Morelle, the
housekeeper, with a lamp in her hand, standing at the entrance.

"Just turn the key in the other door, monsieur, for five minutes, that I may, if anyone
comes, have time to retreat."

Greatly surprised, our hero stepped back,
and locked the door—and then joined the
housekeeper, at the other entrance which
opened into a corridor, seemingly leading to
a private staircase.

"Listen to me, monsieur," said Dame
Morelle, "and pray mind what I say.

"You are going to take my master's lugger
to sea this night. On board this lugger you
will find two men, the one named François
Morelle is my brother. He knows of your intention of seizing the lugger, but the other
does not. Now, when you get on deck, of
course they will be alarmed, at least, one of
them will. Neither you nor the men you have
with you must ill-treat or injure those two men;
but secure them, and put them ashore. Do
you contrive to speak to François Morelle, he
is a pilot, and whatever he tells you to do, be

sure you do it, without fail; do you understand me?"

" Perfectly, dame," returned our hero;
"but how am I to know François Morelle from
the other man."

" He is an old man, monsieur, the other is
young. Ah, monsieur," added the housekeeper,
"I love the English, and so does my brother—
he was a prisoner four years in England, and
a good man shewed him great kindness. My
first mistress, when I was a young woman, was
an English lady. Ah, how good and how
beautiful she was—she married a French
count, and they lived very happily together,
but I must not stop gossipping, for monsieur
will not be long before he comes for you.
Ah, monsieur, he is a good, kind-hearted
man, but his belief in destiny—all the
rage with great men now-a-days — blinds
him.

" Mademoiselle de Morni sends her kind
wishes for your safe arrival in your own

country, and bids you be quite easy about the sweet young creature you leave under her care, and mademoiselle herself sends you this, with a thousand affectionate wishes, and hopes for your safety."

Augustus Chamberlain took the locket sent him by Annie Mortimer, with exceeding emotion and delight. The locket was one given her by Mademoiselle de Morni, and it contained a tress of Annie's hair. It was a beautifully executed piece of jewellery, and set round with pearls.

" I must go, monsieur; it is nearly eleven o'clock, and I would not be discovered for any consideration."

" My dear dame, you have made me quite happy," said our hero. " Pray tell Mademoiselle de Morni that I will never forget her kindness; and tell her who is dearer to me than life, child as she is, that only with life shall this locket be torn from me."

" Eh, bon Dieu ! you are both young lovers,"

said the dame, with a smile, "but may God prosper and join you together again."

Our hero pressed the housekeeper's hand. "Dame," said he, "we may never meet again; but——"

"Hush! I hear a sound—go," and, pulling the door to, she hurried away along the corridor.

Our hero hastened to the door, and quietly unlocked it. Scarcely two minutes afterwards he heard a step—the handle of the door turned, and Monsieur de Hauteville entered the room, carrying a dark lantern in his hand. Our hero put on the pilot coat and cap left for him on the table, and then Monsieur de Hauteville said, "We will now go out through this door," and he walked over to the door Dame Morelle had just closed—"I unbolted and unlocked it to-day purposely."

"It is lucky you did," thought the midshipman, following his host, who threw open the door, and walked along a narrow corridor, passing one or two doors, which opened into other parts of the chateau, no doubt, into Miss Mortimer's chamber and other apartments. A long flight of stairs led to the basement story, and to a number of rooms evidently not then used by the family. They soon reached a door, which Monsieur de Hauteville unlocked, and passed through into a back court; thence they proceeded through another door into the garden.

It was an extremely dark night, the wind apparently blowing fresh, and exceedingly cold. Monsieur de Hauteville took the path across the garden, till he reached the private door, which he unbolted and unlocked. Having both passed out, he simply closed the door, and walked on till they reached the road leading to Pierre Point village and the sea-beach. Then Monsieur de Hauteville paused, and walked abreast with our hero.

"It is a dark night," he said, "but after a time you will get accustomed to it. There is a very good compass in the binnacle on the deck of the lugger, and a lamp underneath. In the little cabin you will find another lamp, and in a cupboard behind the door materials to strike a light. The night is so dark, I would advise you, after running about two leagues to the northward, to lie-to till daylight. My little boat is a fast one; but rather over-masted, and too much canvas; but you are the best judge, being a thorough sailor, and can reduce your canvas to your liking."

"You have been very kind and considerate, Monsieur de Hauteville," said our hero, "and I have no doubt, by following your instruc- tions, we shall get into the Channel without mishap. But where shall I find the three men you spoke of?"

"I will tell you; but first I have a request to make, and that is, in case of any mishap, or your capture in running across Channel, that you will keep my name from becoming known in this transaction, for, in my present position with the government, my conniving at the escape of four English prisoners would be troublesome to me to explain."

"Depend on it, monsieur," returned the midshipman, "I would not, under any circumstances, commit so ungrateful an act. If we are captured, those that take us shall be led to believe that we seized the lugger, and cut her adrift."

"I am quite satisfied," said Monsieur de Hauteville. "Now, as to the three men,—you will find them in a large shed, just off the little pier, where a boat, oars, sails, &c., are usually kept. They are there now awaiting your coming; and believe that they are released owing to your having the power to bribe their jailor. Pray let them think so. Ah, mon Dieu! I had nearly forgotten to tell you that two men sleep every night on board the lugger. However, you can easily manage them—take them by surprise, bind them, and put them into the shed. A night's confinement will do them no harm, and it will have a good appearance. In fact, I do not expect that the slightest enquiry will be made.

" Now, Monsieur Chamberlain, I shall leave you; that path leads direct to the beach and the shed; rest satisfied that every care and attention shall be paid to Miss Mortimer; for whom my niece already feels the affection of a sister."

Monsieur de Hauteville held out his hand. The midshipman took it, and, despite the strange misgivings that agitated his mind, pressed it warmly, saying, " He felt and appreciated his noble generosity, and hoped a time might come when they should meet again." He said no more, for Monsieur de Hauteville appeared uneasy and impatient. Again pressing each other's hands, they separated, Monsieur de Hauteville walking rapidly down the hill towards the chateau.

CHAPTER X.

Augusius Chamberlain remained for a moment standing where Monsieur de Hauteville had left him; he almost hesitating to take the step he had resolved on, but then he thought, " If I do not, a prison awaits me; and the worst that can happen is still a prison." So, hesitating no longer, with a quick step he quickly descended to the beach. He paused at the foot of the hill, and listened; but heard only the sound of the full tide as it broke with a threatening sound upon the rocks, and the rush of the wind as it swept over the hill, and ruffled the water beneath. He could not see either the shed or the lugger, but he knew from his observations during his visit in the daytime, with Monsieur de Hauteville, that the former was not far off. It was a thick, cloudy night, not a star to be seen; still there was neither fog nor mist.

He proceeded about fifty yards towards where he knew the lugger lay, when he heard a voice, not many yards off, and then saw a dark figure standing on the beach. The voice said, " Haul your wind, messmate, and heave to."

" All right," replied our hero, who at once conjectured that here was one of the men he expected to meet. As soon as he spoke, the man came up to him, saying,

" I am so glad your honour's come. Blow me, if I wasn't beginning to fear something was wrong."

" I knew your voice, my man," said our hero. " You must be Tom Darking."

" Yes, your honour, all right. There's Bill and Jim Barker keeping watch the other side of the shed."

" I am so glad, Tom, that you are one of my party, and that the brothers Barker are the others; they are good and steady sea-men. But do not make any noise, for there are two men sleeping in the lugger I intend seizing."

" We'll soon settle their log, your honour; just let me get my claw on their windpipes."

" Yes," returned our hero, with a smile, " I am quite aware, Tom, of your powers in that line; but we must secure these men without hurting them. "

Just then they came to the shed, and joined the two brothers, who were delighted to see our hero, and who were seamen be-longing to the unfortunate Cumberland packet. The four men proceeded down to the pier. They soon perceived the lugger lying moored in the middle of the creek, with warps on each side of the creek, and an anchor ahead.

" Go round, Bill," said our hero to one of the brothers, " and cast off the warps; we shall then be able to haul the lugger alongside the pier, and get on board without noise."

"Aye, aye, sir," and Bill proceeded to execute his duty.

When this was done the lugger was hauled gently alongside, and our hero and Tom Darking sprang on deck. The fore hatch was instantly thrown back, and a man's head and shoulders was raised up, shouting out—

"Tonnerre de Dieu! voleurs! What do you want?"

"Just let me help you up, mounseer," said Tom Darking, seizing the amazed Frenchman, lifting him forcibly out, and turning him over on the deck like a turtle.

"What's the matter? Sacre bleu! What's on deck?" said the other man, who also looked out.

Our hero could see this was the old man François; so he pulled him on deck, whispering, "you are François Morelle."

"Ah, Mon Dieu! Oui."

"Now, Tom, just tie your man's legs and

hands, and carry him ashore to the shed; this man is a pilot. I want to ask him a few questions."

Whilst the three men were carrying the refractory sailor ashore our hero said to François Morell, " what would you advise me to do, to sail out northward ?"

" No, Monsieur; in two hours you would run into the clutches of the cruiser, Sans Pareil, a faster craft than this."

Our hero started.

The old man then said, "attendez vous— when ready to start, steer direct from here, for the south shore. When you make the land, hug it; there's no fear; keep along the coast, and by daylight, with this wind, you will make the West Penmarks. You had better then be guided by your own observations."

" I will follow your advice, mon ami, and God bless those that—"

" Eh, mon Dieu !" hastily interrupted the old man. " I am only answering questions I can't help answering; so bind my hands and legs like my comrade, and put us together in the shed."

Augustus Chamberlain squeezed the old man's hand, but said no more. He was accordingly slightly bound and conveyed on shore by the brothers and left in the shed. Our hero had no time for thought, the tide was falling; so all set vigorously to work to haul in the warps, cast loose the lugs, and warp her out to the buoy. As they were doing so one of the men in the shed began shouting out.

" Blow me, if they won't wake up some lubber or other with their piping," said Tom Darking.

" Not they," replied our hero; " they are a mile and a half from the village, or collection of fishing boats away to the eastward. Now then, stand by and hoist our fore lug; and you, Bill, give her a cast to the southward. I will take the helm."

" How's the wind, sir," asked Tom, "for it's so blessed dark, and the coast scarcely to be seen, that the dickens a bit of me can make out which way the north or south lies."

" The wind's east, Tom; now, up with the lug."

" It's a rasping bit of canvas any how, for such a little craft as this," remarked the two men-of-war's men, " and the breeze is fresh."

" I want to make a run before daylight," said Augustus Chamberlain, " so crack on canvas, I will tell you why by-and-by. Now let go," he sang out, as he grasped the tiller, and away went the lugger under a staggering breeze.

Two great sand banks lay between his course and the West Penmarks, but he had, short as his glance of the little chart in the saloon was, had seen that he could go right over them at that time of tide. There was a neat brass binnacle on deck just before the tiller, and in it a compass and an oil lamp; this Tom Darking lighted from the cabin lamp, and then steering east and by south, he let the lugger dash through the crested billows at the rate of eight knots.

"My eyes, don't she go through the water, Bill," said his brother as they stood in the bows, trying to make out the land under their lee bow.

"I wonder why our skipper is steering this course; for, blow me, if it will take us across the channel."

"Oh, let him alone," said Tom Darking, "he knows what he's about."

"Aye, aye, he's a true blue, that I knows, every inch of him. He's one of the Leander's. Who knows but he is cutting out of the way of one of Johnny Crapaud's cruisers."

Our hero, as he stood at the tiller, and perceived the way the lugger heeled over to the stiff breeze, said to himself, "She's fast, but crank, or rather over-masted, and her sail's too broad in the head for winter weather."

The night was exceedingly dark, and particularly so for an easterly breeze, which, generally speaking, blows with a clear sky.

The further they ran out, and when they had cleared Audierne Head, the stiffer the breeze became, and the sea began to be felt. The object was to make the Penmarks by day-light.

But the breeze kept rapidly increasing—so much so, that our hero was forced to lower the lugs, and reef.

CHAPTER XI.

WITH two reefs in each lug, the lugger not only went steadier but faster, for she did not bury herself.   The sea became exceedingly rough as they ran across the edge of the outer bank, and washed the lugger's decks at times —it was a tumble of a sea, owing to a race of tide.

"Here, Bill," said our hero to the oldest of the brothers, "just you take a spell at the tiller.   Keep to the south of east, and Tom and I will go and rummage the cabin, and see if there is not something aboard to splice the main-brace; for the breeze is sharp enough to render a nip necessary."

"I trust that there is something better than water aboard, your honour—she looks like a yacht, and yachts on our coast ain't remarkable for carrying only water."

"Now, Tom," said the midshipman, "come below."

Our hero had now time to look about him in the cabin. It was small, of course, for twenty tons is a small craft; but the most had been made of the space. The bedding and furniture had all been removed; but a large hamper was standing in a kind of pantry off the cabin stairs. This was, if we except the lamp, the sole article to be seen.

"Well, sir," said Tom, "here's something, at all events," dragging the hamper into the cabin. "I suppose the owner of this here craft is not given to winter cruising—seeing as how he has landed all the rest of his traps. But you won't mind, sir, a night or two without a feather bed under you."

"No, indeed," returned our hero, "we will excuse the beds, if the hamper contains the staff of life." On unpacking it, they found a bag of biscuits, about twenty pounds of raw beef, a dozen bottles of the wine of the country, and half-a-dozen bottles of brandy.

" Well, sir," remarked Tom, with a very satisfied look at the store before him, which he commenced putting into a locker. " This will last us a week, at all events ; and if we are not capsized or taken we can make the English coast in that time."

" If we can find any water," said our hero, " we shall do; though our stores do not boast of variety ; but hunt out a mug or a glass, or anything, that I may serve out a little of this brandy."

" If I had a light, sir, I'd overhaul the forecastle. Mayhap the mounseers we turned adrift may have some crockery in their crib."

" There's flint and steel; I daresay you will find a candle or a lamp in the berth," said our hero, putting one of the bottles of brandy in his pocket, and proceeding on deck.

Tom plunged down into the little confined

fore cuddy of the lugger, and, striking a light, he and one of his comrades inspected the premises. They found a bunch of candles, a pitcher of water, a keg of salt herrings, and three or four loaves of bread. There were two berths, with their bedding, a couple of cutlasses, an old blunderbuss, and a large cow's horn full of powder, and a stock of balls in a bag.

"My eye! Bill, this here blunderbuss is loaded. If the lubbers had only shoved this up and blazed away at us, they'd have shortened some of our logs; blow me if they wouldn't."

"Come along," answered Bill; " here's a couple of mugs, and I'm blessed if I have smelt a glass of grog since our unlucky capture in the Cumberland."

A good mug of brandy all round cheered the whole party, for the night was piercingly cold. It was the latter end of January, and an "easter" on the coast of France at that time of the year is anything but pleasant.

Their situation was too critical for any of the party on board the lugger to turn in for even an hour's rest; for the wind, after two hours run, was evidently inclined to get to the north-east and blow in puffs and in squalls.

"I thought the wind would shift," said our hero to Bill Barker, "by the sky being overcast; it had not the appearance of a true 'easter.'"

"No, sir," returned the sailor; "and it will be sure to end in a westerly gale, the worst that can blow upon this coast. It was a westerly gale that wrecked the seventy-four."

Before the dawn made, the breeze was quite westerly, and just as it became clear enough for our little party to distinguish the West Penmarks, they at the same time made out a large cutter, about five miles to leeward of them, evidently standing out from the Bay of Audierne.

"Ah!" said our hero, "I can now see the necessity of the course we steered. That

cutter is the French cruiser Sans Pareil.
If we had attempted to steer our proper course
to the northward we should undoubtedly have
been captured. As it is, she is nearly five
miles to leeward, and evidently in chase of
us, having been disappointed by our change
of course."

What to do in the face of a rapidly increasing gale, was somewhat puzzling to
those on board the little craft. The sea was
breaking heavily over the whole range of
rocks of the Penmarks, the cutter was between
them and their proper course, whilst, on the
other hand, their vessel was far too small at
that season of the year to stand out and face
the great waves of the Atlantic as they rolled
in from the westward.

The French cutter was carrying a press of
canvas, and appeared to sail remarkably
fast. She was, they judged, about one hundred and twenty tons burden. In this dilemma,
after consulting with Bill Barker, an old and
experienced sailor, who agreed that the lugger

was quite unfit to contend with the weather, which was rapidly freshening into a gale, our hero resolved to run round the Penmark rocks, and get out of sight of the cutter. He would make for the East Penmarks, and anchor under the lee of the large island of Glonant, where there was good holding ground, and shelter from west and south-west wind. It was not likely that the cutter would suspect them of doing this.

Slacking sheet, after weathering the West Penmarks, they ran on, carrying all the canvas they dared, in order to gain their anchorage before the cutter could weather the Penmarks and sight them.

Making their breakfast of biscuit and wine, they carried on till they rounded, about midday, the Island of Glonant. There was not a single fishing boat or lugger of any kind to be seen in the little bay they ran into, just as the gale freshened in right earnest. The sea in this sheltered bight was perfectly smooth. There was no battery or residence on this barren rocky island, so anchoring, they lowered their sails, and made themselves snug.

"I think we shall be safe now, sir," said Bill Barker. "I know the place well; the cutter will scarcely venture, in this gale, to run into so dangerous a position. We ran in here one night in a dense fog in the Nautilus, ten-gun brig, and escaped by a miracle, being on the end of the island. We did not know exactly where we were, for we had chased two merchant brigs, and were caught in the fog before we could look out; but our skipper, finding he had run into smooth water, and the lead giving ten fathoms, he anchored. We rode out a heavy gale of forty-eight hours, and when the fog cleared, we saw where we were, and what a narrow escape we had had."

About an hour after anchoring, the gale shifted into the south-west, blowing harder, and a thick drizzling rain falling, that shut out the mainland from their view.

Our hero considered, doubtful and precarious as their situation was, that they were safe from the pursuit of the "Sans Pareil" cutter, which would probably be forced to make for Brest harbour for shelter.

Tom and one of the Barkers, caring very little about their situation, commenced preparations for making a dinner off some of the beef.

Our hero was pacing the short deck, and thinking of poor Annie Mortimer's melancholy position, when a dark object caught his attention to leeward of them; the next moment the sound of a cable running out rapidly through the hawse-hole of a vessel attracted the attention of all in the lugger.

"By Jove!" said Augustus Chamberlain, "there's an anchor let go by some craft to leeward of us. Hark! I hear men's voices, and now I think I can make out the indistinct outline of a vessel. If it's the Sans Pareil, it's all up with us."

"It may be a merchant craft bound into St. Gurdoff, which port is not more than six miles under our lee," said Bill Barker.

Presently the fog lifted a little with the increasing breeze, and all distinctly made out the raking masts of a large schooner, but not her hull. The next moment the fog closed round her again.

"Well," said our hero, " it's not the cutter, at all events. Now it strikes me, we might make ourselves master of that craft, to-night, if she's a merchantman, and not a privateer."

The idea of seizing a fine schooner, probably well laden, roused the spirits of the little party to enthusiasm. They did not care a rush for the risk of life. The boldness of the project was just the very thing to suit their reckless natures.

"We can drop down on them during the night," said Tom Darking. "We have the blunderbuss and lots of balls, and can rig out three boarding pikes in no time."

The midshipman thought it a very possible adventure to achieve, provided the schooner was a merchant craft. French she was sure to be, for no English merchant vessel would ever run into such a place and anchor. He calculated, by the short glimpse he had of the schooner, that she was about a hundred and fifty, or a hundred and sixty tons. If so, she would have probably not more than eight or ten men on board. During the night there would not be more than the watch on deck. He was well aware what a surprise could do. He had joined in many a daring thing of the kind, and with greater peril to incur, and having thought over it well, and eaten his share of a piece of boiled beef and biscuit, washed down by some tolerable wine, he held a consultation in the cabin with his very limited, but most determined crew.

" She is dead to leeward of us, sir," observed Bill Barker. " We need only haul in the slack of our cable and drop down on her; we shall be on her deck before they know anything about us. Your honour speaks their lingo like mounseer himself, and if they do hail us, you can say we are a fishing lugger broke adrift, and ask them to throw us a rope. Once aboard, we'll make short work of it."

"Well, your idea is not a bad one," replied our hero; "so go and get the gun in the fore cabin, and rig out the two boat hooks into boarding pikes; these and the two old but very heavy cutlasses, will furnish us with arms. But I feel quite satisfied that eight or ten unarmed men, taken by surprise, will offer very little resistance."

"There's a large horn lantern, sir, down forward," said Tom; "we shall want it when on the schooner's deck; till then we can cover it with a piece of canvas."

When the blunderbuss was brought to our hero he had it loaded with six balls, and then confided it to the care of Bill Barker, who he knew would not use it recklessly.

"If we can take the schooner without bloodshed, so much the better."

As the sun went down the gale moderated a little, but the fog continued exceedingly dense.

About midnight a cup of brandy was served out all round, and then the two Barkers went forward and commenced hauling in the slack of the cable; the anchor soon broke ground, and the lugger was permitted to drift slowly before the wind. Almost immediately they perceived the faint glimmer of a lantern evidently hoisted at the mast head of the schooner.

"All right, sir," said Tom Darking, "we are dropping right upon her."

As they approached nearer, they were startled by hearing either shouts or yells, proceeding from the strange vessel.

"My eyes! sir," said Tom, "what are they up to."

The lugger was checked, and all anxiously listened. A number of voices were heard yelling a drunken chorus.

"They are holding a drunken bout," remarked our hero. "Hark, how they yell and shout."

"I'm blowed if there aint a legion of devils

in her," said Tom, who was holding a boat hook to grapple with the stranger, as soon as they came near enough.

The uproar was evidently in the cabin of the schooner. Some voices were singing, and then others joined in with yells and drunken screams.

As they caught a nearer view of the schooner, our hero, in a whisper, said to Tom, " she's a privateer."

" The devil she is," cried Tom, " then sir, we're in for a spree," and hitching in the rigging they brought the lugger alongside, without noise or shock ; indeed the gale howled through the rigging, with such shrill noises, knocking about some loose blocks, that those half drunk in the cabin were not likely to be disturbed in their orgies. There was not a soul to be seen on deck. Our hero sprung lightly over the bulwarks followed by Tom Darking with the lantern; a strong light came through the skylight of the cabin, from which also arose loud laughter, shouts, and thumping of tables.

In the middle of the schooner was a formidable long eighteen-pound carronade, working on a half circle. As Tom turned the lantern forward, our hero started, for he perceived a human form lying on the deck; and approaching he saw a man tied hand and foot, and fastened to two ring bolts in the deck. The man, a tall well attired seaman, let his eyes rest upon our hero saying, " Good God, are you English."

" Yes," replied our hero, " how is this?"

" Cut me loose sir, for God's sake; there are three men tied in this manner upon the deck, and thirteen in the forehold. Cut us all loose, and we will help you to take this accursed craft. There are two females, mother and daughter, in the cabin, and when these ruffians get blind and furiously drunk, they will destroy them, and doubtless murder us."

" Hark!" exclaimed our hero, cutting at the

same time the stranger's cords, "they are wildly drunk."

"Let your men come with me," said the stranger, with the lantern, "I will free my messmates; you see in this boat there are boarding pikes in abundance. There are only five-and-twenty below, and we can master them."

"Well, release your comrades quickly," said our hero, "I am an officer of His Majesty's ship Leander."

"We will obey you implicitly," observed the stranger. "I was mate of a privateer. and my comrades have stout hearts and willing hands."

The two Barkers went with the mate, and cast off the fore hatch, after cutting loose the three men most cruelly and brutally bound to ring bolts. Whilst anxiously listening, our hero heard a piercing shriek, the agonized cry of a female, arose from the cabin, followed by loud shouts. Snatching up the blunderbuss, he rushed to the cabin skylight,

dashed in the glass, and shouted out, " Mis-
creants, yield to the crew of a British frigate,"
and through the smashed glass, he beheld a
scene of indescribable confusion.   Some
twenty men were seated in various attitudes
round a very large cabin, the table in the
centre covered with a profusion of eat-
ables and drinkables.   Two ruffians were
dragging a girl into the main cabin from
a smaller one, and two others were holding a tall, robust, woman who struggled
violently; but the moment the glass of the
sky-light was smashed in, the tables were
overturned, the lights dashed out, and a furious
rush made up the cabin stairs, first firing
several pistol shots through the sky-light.

" Now, Tom," shouted our hero, " stand
firm, our comrades are coming up from the
fore-hold." The first men that rushed up from
the cabin fell before the discharge of the
blunderbuss, and then our hero and Tom
cut away with their cutlasses. Still the crowd
of frantic half-drunken privateer's men

forced their way up, several having battle
lanterns in their hands, lighted, which they
hooked into the main rigging. Fighting despe-
rately, though forced backwards, our hero
and Tom tried to keep their ground. The
tables were turned, the released prisoners,
armed with boarding pikes and hatchets, with
a true English cheer, charged into the midst
of the infuriated Frenchmen, who fiercely
shouted, " no quarter," " scélérats Anglais,"
" massacre them !"

A tall, powerful man, the captain of the
privateer, led them fiercely against their determined enemies. Several on both sides had
fallen, when Augustus Chamberlain made a
desperate rush and faced the privateer
captain.

" Ah ! chien Anglais," said the captain,
" take this," and down came his heavy cutlass, intending to cut down our hero, but
Tom Darking's pike caught the blow, and
the young midshipman drove him back.
A furious contest took place, till a terrible

blow from our hero's cutlass across the throat, stretched the privateer skipper mortally wounded on the skylight. This blow evidently decided the fight, the Privateer's men broke, some threw themselves overboard, and others jumping into the lugger alongside cut her adrift, Tom and the stranger who fought furiously, were going to jump into the lugger after them, but our hero shouted to them to let them go; there had been slaughter enough.

The mate of the English privateer, Fox, coming up to our hero, said,

"It has been sharp work, sir; your killing that villain Pierre Malin finished the fight. you are wounded, sir."

"Nothing of any consequence," replied the midshipman. "I see you have had a cut or two yourself; how many of your men have fallen, and how many are wounded."

It was a fierce fight, certainly, though of short duration. Seven Frenchmen lay stark and stiff upon the deck, beside their Captain.

Not a single wounded one remained. Four Englishmen were killed, and five wounded. Jem Barker was slightly wounded, and his brother's head was cut from the blow of a pike. Our hero had two cuts from a cutlass, one slight one on the head, and another rather deep one on the left shoulder.

The dead were instantly consigned to that so oft resting-place of the gallant seamen, the wounded taken away into the fore cabin, whilst the living began clearing the deck, and washing away the horrid traces of the fight. The mate of the Fox, having washed away the blood from his face, joined our hero, who was doing the same thing.

" You have taken the fastest privateer in the Channel, sir, and you have also slain the greatest ruffian that ever sailed under a privateer flag. Had we not better go down into the cabin, and relieve the fears of the unfortunate women, who owe their lives to your gallantry and courage? You have a powerful arm, sir, or you could not have beaten down that great brute, Pierre Malin, with a single blow."

" You and your men, mate, fought as gallantly as men could fight. Pray to what vessel did you belong, and who are the women we have so fortunately rescued?"

" I was first mate, sir, of the Fox privateer, and the two females in the cabin were the wife and daughter-in-law of the unfortunate skipper of the Fox. He was cruelly slain after the fight was over, in cold blood, by the rascal you slew. When we get to rights I will tell you, sir, all the particulars. This schooner is the celebrated Belle Poule, which has evaded all our cruisers by her speed and audacity."

" Belle Poule!" exclaimed the midshipman. " How strange."

Our hero called Tom Darking to bring a lantern, and then all three descended into the cabin. They paused at the door, whilst Tom opened the lantern, and threw a light upon the strange scene within. The cabin was a

very large one. Two swinging lamps were
suspended from the ceiling, but the lights
were extinguished, and the glasses smashed.
The table was overturned and lay broken, on
the floor strewed with meat, bread, wine, jars
of brandy, and various other articles. The
sides of the cabin were ornamented with fire-
arms, tastefully arranged. As they looked
upon this scene, the face of a girl protruded
from the open door of a small private sleeping-
berth, gazed at them; and immediately
called out—" Oh, God be praised! It is you,
Mr. Hawkins, then we are saved. My poor
mother is nearly dead. Pray get a light, and
a little water for her."

" Yes, thank God! you are saved," replied
the person addressed, " thanks to this gallant
gentleman;" and, stooping, he picked up a
glass and a bottle of wine. Our hero started
when he heard the voice of the girl, who
came into the cabin to take the tumbler of
wine from the mate. Tom, in the mean-

time, had lighted one of the lamps; and as Augustus stood with his face towards the young girl, she let her glance rest upon his features.

"Ah!" she exclaimed, letting the wine fall, "Am I dreaming?" and she caught hold of the door-post, extremely agitated.

Our hero, surprised and puzzled, looked her earnestly in the face, when the girl, said "Yes, I am now sure. Pray tell me, is not your name Chamberlain?"

"Yes," returned our hero, with a start, and advancing, he looked earnestly into the pale but very interesting face of the young girl, "My name is Augustus Chamberlain, and surely you must be my once little playfellow, Rose Talbot?"

"Ah! thank God, then! We are saved, and by you. Yes; I am Rose Talbot," and the tears rolled down her cheeks as she clasped his hand, and covered it with tears and kisses. "Come in and see my poor mother, who loved you as a son, and who will revive when she knows who, under Providence, saved us from a cruel villain and his associates."

Greatly surprised and affected, Augustus Chamberlain, with a tumbler of wine in his hand, entered the little cabin, followed by Rose.

Stretched upon a mattress on a kind of raised sofa, he beheld Rose's mother, looking fearfully pale, and apparently fainting. When placed under her care, a boy of eight years, he had learned to love Mrs. Talbot as a mother, and Rose as a sister. She raised her head when she saw her favourite, and, taking a little of the wine, she said, "Oh, my dear, dear boy. How blessed I am that Providence has sent one I love so well to save my child."

Our hero stooped down, and kissed the cheek of the lady with real affection.

"Thank God, mother, that I and my

gallant comrades arrived in time. Make your mind easy--we are all right now. Drink this, and be composed. Your persecutors have received their reward."

" Ah, my son, the villains slew my poor husband, in cold blood, and would, but for you, have destroyed us."

" Well, dear mother," said Rose, soothingly, " think no more of the horrors we have gone through. What has passed cannot be recalled. We have brave protectors now, and, please God, we shall get once more to England." She held the wine to her mother's lips, who drank some, and then fell back exhausted.

" She will recover this shock, dear Rose," said our hero, before morning. " I must leave her to your care, as we have a great deal to do before day-light surprises us."

" We shall do very well now, Augustus" said Rose, affectionately pressing his hand, "I have found a brother, and my mother a son; so we have much to thank God for."

Leaving Rose happy and calm to attend to her mother, our hero ascended upon deck.

END OF VOL. I.

T. C. Newby, 30, Welleck Street, Cavendish Square, London.

www.ingramcontent.com/pod-product-compliance
Lightning Source LLC
Chambersburg PA
CBHW021056030726
47496CB00006B/1861